Urban Desires

By: Jodi Chow

A Madame Bovary Retelling

Urban Desires

Jodi Chow

Published by Jodi Chow, 2024.

This is a work of fiction. Similarities to real people, places, or events are entirely coincidental.

URBAN DESIRES

First edition. July 3, 2024.

Copyright © 2024 Jodi Chow.

ISBN: 979-8227246011

Written by Jodi Chow.

To:

My illustrious and gorgeous husband, Paul Chow. Know that in order to write this adulterous novel I had to use pure imagination and research. You have my undying embers of love and devotion. All honor is yours.

Tacoma, Washington 2024 Jodi Chow

This modern retelling of Madame Bovary fast forwards to a world 200 years after the original work. Based in New York-not France- the mundane and repetitive nature of life is still harshly faced and critiqued by Emma Bovary, the great-great-great-granddaughter of the original adulterous farmgirl.

Emma Bovary's life appears perfect on the surface: a lucrative career, a stylish apartment in Brooklyn, and a well-respected husband, Franz, who is a kind-hearted but somewhat dull doctor. However, Emma's restless spirit craves excitement and passion that her routine urban life fails to provide.

While attending a high-profile industry event, Emma meets Léon, a charming and creative man of mystery. They quickly form a deep connection, sharing a love for marketing, music, and the finer things in life. Léon is captivated by Emma's intelligence and beauty, and they begin a dance of intrigue.

She dives into her past to redeem her present. On a trip to Paris, she realizes the mistakes of her mother, but in duality she learns from these mistakes. Standing in front of the Eiffel Tower, she discovers a universal truth. Will the enormity of the situation prove to be too much pressure or will it be perceived for what it is- immense power? Emma is faced with an unknown future. Will she give it her all, or will she yield to nature's unending mysteries?

In the end, Emma Bovary emerges as a stronger, more self-aware woman who understands that true happiness comes from within. *Urban Desires* is a story of love, ambition, and self-discovery, capturing the essence of a modern woman navigating the complexities of life and love in a fast-paced urban environment.

Will seeing the hard truths of life and the unintentional nature of the world inspire her or destroy her? Join Emma as she waits to die.

Part 1

In Brooklyn's heart, where the skyline's bright, I stand on the eve of my wedding night. With a fluttering heart and a wavering sigh, I ponder my future and question why.

Franz, my love, so gentle and refined, with a brilliant mind that's one of a kind. His touch, a promise of tender care, yet something stirs, a rumble that I may stumble into a subtle snare.

Intelligent, brave, a doctor so true, in his eyes, a world I should pursue. But deep within, a whispering fear, a shadow of doubt that's ever near.

In our stylish apartment, dreams take flight, yet my heart feels heavy on this starry night. Is it the weight of vows to come? Or a longing for a life that's just begun?

I see our future, clear and bright, and in the silence I hear that everything will be alright. Am I destined for joy, or bound to stray? On this threshold of love, an eternity of hope to pay.

Brooklyn's streets hum a lullaby sweet, as I stand alone, my thoughts entreat. To Franz, my love, I'll give my all, but will I rise or will I fall? With a heart full of hope and a touch of dread, I step toward the path that lies ahead. For tomorrow, we'll wed, our fates entwine, In this city of dreams, where stars align.

The clouds hung low over New York City, casting a gray pallor over the bustling streets. It was a dreary fall afternoon, the kind that makes everything seem a little more somber, a little less hopeful. Emma Bovary, a modern woman, stood in front of the mirror in her Park Stone Brooklyn brownstone, adjusting the peplum-fitted white wedding gown that just touched her ankles. The dress was elegant yet understated, a nod to a classic era with a sophisticated twist. She couldn't help but feel like a modern-day Marilyn Monroe, but without the red lipstick, bleach, or reputation.

Dark humor played at the corners of her mouth as she imagined her mother watching her, shaking her head in disapproval. "This is it, Emma," she whispered to herself. "Your big day. Try not to look too excited."

With a final glance in the mirror, she grabbed her bouquet of Metropolitan Market roses and made her way to City Hall, or was it City Haul? She hated thinking about going into a government building with the lack of care most citizens showed. It made running into a worker in a bad mood almost impossible to avoid. No matter, she had a marriage to participate in. She straightened her clothes and tried not to think about this occasion as if she were a clown in a world-class circus. Taking a final look, and then heading outside into the fresh wet air, she let her heels clank rhythmically against the sidewalk. The streets of New York seemed indifferent to her journey, the usual cacophony of honking horns and chatter providing a dissonant soundtrack to her thoughts.

As she entered City Hall, the cold marble floors and stark lighting only heightened her sense of unease. Franz stood there, waiting for her patiently in a blue suit that was slightly too big for his large frame. His eyes lit up when he saw her, but the sparkle quickly faded to a look of quiet resignation. They both knew this wasn't a fairy tale. With hushed whispers and muted excitement, they stood before the judge.

Emma stood facing the stand where a tired looking man with white hair sat. Her slender body moved slightly towards Franz. He cupped her delicately manicured hands in his. Normally at this time, he would be in the operating room holding someone's heart, but today he was holding his- Emma blushed knowing that it was her. The judge smiled at their physical differences. She was slender and short while he was voluminous and bulky. The judge laughed as he helped the couple tie the knot. The ceremony was brief, efficient—*just like everything else in this city*, Emma thought. The judge's monotone voice echoed in the cavernous hall, a stark contrast to the vows of eternal love and commitment he recited. Emma glanced at Franz, who offered her a small, reassuring smile. They both knew it wasn't passion that brought them here, but practicality.

A smile crossed her lips at the redundancy of it all. When the judge pronounced them husband and wife, Franz leaned in and kissed her. It was a polite, almost obligatory kiss, lacking the fiery passion of romance novels. Emma closed her eyes and tried to summon some emotion, but all she felt was a strange mix of relief and trepidation. After the ceremony, they walked out into the crisp autumn air. The sky was still overcast, the threat of rain hanging in the air. Franz took her hand, and they made their way to IHOP for brunch. It was a fittingly mundane end to their unremarkable wedding day, Emma thought with scorn. Doing her best not to unleash her rage on Franz, the waitress came over quickly and greeted them with a forced smile. Emma knew the drill, she sat stalk still and they ordered pancakes and coffee. The syrupy sweetness of the pancakes did little to mask the bitter taste of reality.

Franz checked his watch frequently, clearly anxious about returning to the hospital. Emma sipped her coffee and stared out the window, watching the world go by. They exchanged a few words, and they mostly ate in silence. It wasn't an uncomfortable silence, but it wasn't the comfortable kind either. It was the silence of two people who knew they had made a decision and were now dealing with the consequences. Franz, satisfied, made the uncomfortable first move to begin exiting their booth. Feeling full and ready to leave, Emma grabbed her soft pink overcoat and grumbled in her seat.

When the check came, Franz paid, and they stood to leave. He kissed her on the cheek and promised to be home by dinner. Emma watched him walk away, his figure quickly swallowed by the crowd. She stood there for a moment, feeling a strange sense of loss. Then, with a sigh, she turned and headed back to her apartment. As she walked through the city, the weight of her decision settled on her shoulders. She wasn't sure what the future held, but she knew one thing: this was her life now. No turning back, no second chances. In the colorful library of her city dwelling, Emma Bovary found herself utterly overwhelmed by the dusty volumes that lined the shelves. Many books whispered secrets of a bygone era, holding within its pages the tales of her illustrious lineage. Her fingers traced the spines delicately, as if afraid to disturb the echoes of the past that lingered in the air. Her past wasn't a fairytale or beautiful. It was dark and disillusioned, marked with chaos and betrayal. Breathing in a deep sigh, she let the weight of the world escape her lips.

It was here, amidst the leather-bound tomes and the soft glow of antique lamps, that Emma discovered a hidden diary belonging to her great- great-grandmother, Berthe Bovary. It seemed like fate that she found it on this special occasion. The yellowed pages revealed a life of daring escapades and forbidden romances, chronicling Berthe's journey from a stifling existence in provincial France to the bustling streets of New York during the strife before World War I.

As Emma read, she felt a kinship with Berthe, whose yearning for freedom and passion mirrored her own. Emma looked up from the pages and silently cursed to herself. She had been such a baby. The brownstone was a gift from her mother who inherited it from her mother, who got it from Berthe. Her whole life, Emma always measured Grandma Berthe's successes to her own. This kept her sharp, but also unsteady. Accepting her new life, she continued to read.

As the shadows of World War I loomed over France, young Berthe Bovary found herself in desperate circumstances. Her mother, also named Berthe, was left orphaned and destitute after her mother's tragic suicide. Her father, the town's doctor, slowly fell into ruin. No one in Yonville gave two shakes about Berthe, so she was sent to live in an orphanage. She spent her life in poverty and died of the affliction. The younger Berthe was then left alone in the world just like her mother.

Berthe woke up before dawn, shivering under a thin, worn blanket. The wooden bed creaked as she sat up, rubbing her eyes and looking around the dimly lit room. There was no one to greet her, no mother to offer a warm smile or a father to ruffle her hair. The silence was her only companion.

She pulled on her ragged dress and threadbare shawl, slipping her small feet into oversized clogs. The shoes clunked awkwardly as she moved about the small space, gathering her meager possessions for the day ahead. In the corner of the room, a small iron stove barely provided enough heat to cook a simple meal. Berthe lit a fire with trembling hands, using the last bits of kindling she had collected from the forest. A thin porridge simmered on the stove, its meager aroma filling the tiny room. She ate quickly, knowing that every moment of daylight was precious.

Arriving in the village, Berthe headed to the market square, hoping to find some work. The vendors knew her situation and sometimes took pity on her, offering small tasks in exchange for food or a few coins. Today, Madame Lefevre, the baker's wife, allowed Berthe to sweep the floors and clean the baking trays. It was hard work, but the promise of a loaf of bread at the end of the day kept her motivated.

Her fingers ached from the cold and the scrubbing, but Berthe worked diligently, determined to earn her keep. She listened to the villagers' gossip, hearing snippets of a world that seemed so distant from her own struggles. They spoke of dances, harvests, and family feuds, while Berthe's world was a constant battle for survival.

Tears welled in her eyes, but she brushed them away, determined not to succumb to despair. She knew she had to be strong, had to keep going, if only for the hope that someday, somehow, things might get better. As sleep finally claimed her, Berthe dreamed of a better life, one where she was not defined by her poverty or her orphaned status.

Berthe's life took a drastic turn when a sailor named Lucien came into her village.

Berthe's first tale was of her youth in rural France, where her beauty caught the eye of a wealthy soldier, Lucien. Their courtship was swift, a whirlwind of stolen glances and secret rendezvous. Yet, beneath the surface of their romance, there was an undercurrent of tension. Lucien's family disapproved of Berthe, seeing her as nothing more than a poor orphan unworthy of their son. Despite their bitter hearts, Lucien married Berthe and brought her to New York.

Lucien, a rugged yet kind-hearted man, had been stationed in France as part of the American Expeditionary Forces. Moved by Berthe's plight and captivated by her striking resemblance to the Virgin Mary, he struck a deal with the local authorities. With promises of a better life in America, Lucien convinced them to allow him to take Berthe with him.

Berthe, with nothing tying her to her homeland and intrigued by the prospect of a new beginning, embarked on a tumultuous journey across the Atlantic with just a suitcase and a letter from her grandmother Emma. Lucien, true to his word, cared for Berthe during the voyage, shielding her from the horrors of war that raged around them.

Upon reaching America, Berthe found herself in a new world of opportunity and challenges. Lucien settled in a bustling port city, where Berthe struggled to adapt to the language and customs. Despite the initial hardships, Berthe's resilient spirit and determination allowed her to flourish in her new surroundings.

Years later, as Berthe reflected on her journey from the quiet French countryside to the bustling streets of America, she often thought of her grandmother, Emma, and the tragic legacy that had shaped her own path.

She was terrified of leaving her miserable life in France, but Berthe, with her indomitable spirit, did not wallow in despair. Instead, she transformed her sorrow into a steely resolve. She left her village, moving to the bustling city of Brooklyn where she reinvented herself. She became a sought-after seamstress, her designs adorning the elite of American society. The year was 1922, and America was roaring with prosperity and opportunity. The brownstone Lucien had his eye on stood proudly on a tree-lined street, its red-brick façade and wrought-iron railings exuding a sense of stability and permanence.

He approached the building, heart pounding with a mix of excitement and apprehension. The realtor, a sharp-dressed man with a thin mustache, greeted him with a firm handshake and a smile that spoke of deals closed and futures secured. Lucien had saved every penny from his job in the military, working tirelessly to afford this piece of the American dream.

Inside, the brownstone was everything he had hoped for. High ceilings, large windows that let in streams of sunlight, and enough space to start a family and maybe even a business. Lucien signed the papers with a sense of finality, his name now tied to his family's success.

Meanwhile, Berthe's life had taken a turn for the better. After years of struggle and hardship, she had found her niche in the vibrant community of Brooklyn. Her skills as a seamstress, honed in the quiet desperation of her youth, had become her ticket to success. The early 1920s were a time of fashion and flapper dresses, and Berthe's delicate handiwork and eye for detail were in high demand.

She started small, sewing for neighbors and friends, but word of her talent spread quickly. Soon, she had regular clients from all over the borough, women who came to her for custom dresses, intricate alterations, and fashionable accessories. Her little workshop, set up in the parlor of the brownstone, was a hive of activity. Fabrics of every color and texture filled the space, and the hum of the sewing machine was a constant background noise.

In the spring of 1920, Berthe gave birth to her first and only child, a daughter named Stella. The brownstone, once echoing with the sounds of construction and business, now also resonated with the soft cries of a newborn. Stella was a tiny bundle of joy, with her mother's dark eyes and her father's determined spirit.

Berthe balanced her growing business with the demands of motherhood, finding a rhythm in the chaos. Stella often slept in a bassinet beside the sewing table, lulled to sleep by the rhythmic clatter of the sewing machine. Berthe's clients would coo over the baby, bringing little gifts and offering advice.

Lucien and Berthe's hard work began to pay off. The brownstone became a symbol of their success and resilience. Lucien, ever the entrepreneur, started a small carpentry business on the side, using his skills to craft custom furniture for the growing number of new homeowners in the area. His pieces, known for their craftsmanship and durability, quickly gained popularity.

Berthe's seamstress business continued to thrive. She hired two young women to help with the increasing workload, transforming her parlor into a full-fledged atelier. The demand for her dresses and alterations grew, and she began to receive commissions from wealthier clients in Manhattan.

Despite their newfound prosperity, the past still lingered in Berthe's mind. The hardships of her childhood, the poverty, and the loneliness were shadows that sometimes darkened her bright new life. But with Lucien by her side and Stella in her arms, she found the strength to push those memories aside.

She worked tirelessly not only to provide for her family but to create a legacy. Berthe wanted Stella to grow up with the opportunities she never had, to be proud of her heritage and her parents' hard work. She taught her daughter the values of resilience, creativity, and independence.

In their Brooklyn neighborhood, the family became well-respected members of the community. Neighbors admired their hard work and determination. Berthe was known as a talented seamstress and a loving mother, while Lucien was respected for his craftsmanship and business acumen. They attended local church services, community events, and were active participants in the cultural tapestry of their neighborhood. The brownstone, once just a house, became a home filled with love, laughter, and the promise of a brighter future.

When Stella became of age, she decided to skip the altar boys and go straight for the money. Stella, not keen on getting married, found love in a man named Antoine. He was a French man living in Boston, running a bank, and Stella fell head over heels for his boyish charm. However, Antoine was a man of many secrets. One night, as they strolled along the Seine on a business trip, he confessed to Stella that he was already married. His wife, a frail woman of considerable wealth, lived secluded in their country estate. Stella was devastated, yet she could not bring herself to end their affair. The forbidden nature of their relationship only intensified their bond, but it was not sustainable. When Antoine's wife discovered their liaison, she confronted Stella, offering her a substantial sum to leave Antoine and never return.

Stella was sitting in a small, dimly lit café on the outskirts of Paris, her fingers tapping nervously against the delicate porcelain cup. She had chosen a table in the corner, away from prying eyes, hoping to find a semblance of solace in the hustle and bustle of the city. The 1940s were a time of both glamour and struggle, and Stella had tasted a bit of both.

Her thoughts were interrupted by the sharp click of heels on the tiled floor. She looked up to see a frail yet elegantly dressed woman approaching her. The woman's eyes, though sunken and tired, burned with a fierce determination. This was Antonie's wife, Marguerite, a woman of considerable wealth and influence.

"Stella, I presume?" Marguerite's voice was cold, devoid of the warmth that one might expect from such a refined exterior.

Stella nodded, her heart pounding in her chest. "Yes, that's me."

Marguerite sat down without invitation, her movements deliberate and controlled. She placed a neatly folded handkerchief on the table, smoothing it with meticulous care before looking Stella straight in the eye.

"You know why I'm here," Marguerite began, her voice low and trembling slightly, though her composure remained intact. "I know about you and my husband. I know everything."

Stella swallowed hard, her mind racing. She had feared this moment but had never truly prepared for it. "I...I didn't mean for things to get out of hand," she stammered. "I love him."

Marguerite's laugh was bitter, a sound that echoed with years of pent-up frustration and hurt. "Love? What do you know of love, child? You've known him for a fleeting moment. I've spent my life with him, stood by him through every triumph and every failure."

Stella lowered her gaze, shame washing over her. "I'm sorry," she whispered. "I didn't mean to hurt anyone."

The older woman sighed, her expression softening just a fraction. "Perhaps not. But you have. And now we must deal with the consequences."

She reached into her elegant handbag and pulled out a checkbook. "I understand you are pregnant," she said, her tone matter-of-fact. "This complicates things. However, I am prepared to offer you a substantial sum of money to leave my husband alone. To go back to wherever it is you came from and never return."

Stella felt a lump form in her throat. She was carrying Antonie's child, a child conceived out of love—or what she thought was love. But the reality of her situation was harsh and unforgiving. "How much?" she asked, her voice barely above a whisper.

Marguerite's eyes gleamed with a murderous resolve. "Enough to ensure you and your child are taken care of. Enough to start a new life, far away from here."

Stella hesitated, the weight of the decision pressing down on her. She knew that accepting the money meant giving up any hope of a future with Antonie. But what kind of future would she have if she stayed? Living in the shadows, always the other woman, never truly accepted or loved.

Finally, she nodded. "Alright. I'll go."

Marguerite scribbled a figure on the check, tore it out, and placed it gently on the table in front of Stella. "Take this," she said. "And leave tonight. For your own sake, and for the sake of your child."

Stella picked up the check, her hands trembling. The amount was more than she had ever dreamed of. She looked up at Marguerite, tears welling in her eyes. "Thank you," she said softly.

Marguerite stood, her expression unreadable. "Just go, Stella. And never look back."

Stella watched as the older woman walked away, her back straight and her head held high. She knew that this encounter would haunt her for the rest of her life. But for now, she had to think of her child. She had to start anew.

That night, Stella boarded a train back to Brooklyn, the check clutched tightly in her hand. She had a new life to build, far from the glamour and heartbreak of Paris. And as the train chugged along the tracks, she whispered a silent farewell to Antonie and the dreams she had once held dear.

She came back to the brownstone where she spent every last dollar she was given by the colicky wife to make her nest her own. Stella's return to the brownstone was a triumphant declaration of her independence, but her father had passed away while she was gone. The brownstone, nestled in the heart of Brooklyn, had always been a sanctuary for the family, a place where dreams were nurtured and identities were forged. After her mother, Berthe, moved out into a nursing home, Stella was determined to make it her own, to transform it into a reflection of her personality and aspirations. She poured every last dollar she had been given by Antoine's insufferable wife into the renovation, sparing no expense in her quest to create a lavish and eclectic home.

The first thing she did was to strip the walls of their dull, aging wallpaper, replacing it with rich, deep hues. The living room was adorned with opulent, dark emerald green velvet drapes that cascaded from ceiling to floor, framing large bay windows that let in just the right amount of sunlight. The walls were painted in a sophisticated shade of charcoal gray, providing a perfect backdrop for her collection of vintage gold-framed mirrors and abstract art pieces. A grand crystal chandelier hung from the ceiling, its prisms casting delicate rainbows across the room whenever the light hit them just right.

Stella's furniture was a mix of classic elegance and modern flair. A plush, velvet Chesterfield sofa in a striking shade of royal blue took center stage, complemented by an array of colorful, patterned throw pillows. A sleek, glass coffee table sat in front of it, adorned with art books, fresh flowers, and an assortment of quirky decorative items she had picked up from her travels. The hardwood floors were covered with a Persian rug in rich reds and blues, adding warmth and texture to the space.

The kitchen was a culinary dream, with glossy white cabinets, marble countertops, and state-of-the-art stainless steel appliances. A large, farmhouse-style sink stood in front of a window overlooking a small but charming backyard garden, where Stella planned to grow her own herbs and flowers. She added a touch of whimsy with a collection of colorful, mismatched ceramic plates and bowls displayed on open shelves, and a vintage red Smeg refrigerator that stood out like a bold statement piece.

Starting out on her own again was both exhilarating and daunting for Stella. She reveled in the freedom to make her own decisions, to create a space that was entirely hers. She threw herself into her work as a freelance designer, her creativity flourishing in her new environment.

She only spoke to Berthe when absolutely necessary, maintaining a delicate balance between their relationship and her own need for independence. Stella's brownstone became a haven of inspiration and beauty, a testament to her resilience and her unwavering commitment to living life on her own terms.

Eventually, Stella gave birth to Sylvia, Emma's mother. Emma was now poring over these tales of her ancestors. As Emma read, she felt a deep connection to the women who came before her. She saw their courage, their flaws, and their unyielding pursuit of love and happiness.

Brooklyn in the 1940s was a melting pot of hopes, dreams, and a fair amount of societal constraints, especially for a single mother who was both wealthy and determined to carve out her own destiny. Stella, freshly returned from Paris with a large sum of hush money and a belly full of secrets, found herself navigating this labyrinth with a mix of dark humor and unrelenting resolve. Her neighbors, a curious mix of nosy old ladies and self-righteous housewives, were quick to label her as "that woman," a title spoken in hushed tones over garden fences and in the corners of knitting circles.

"Can you believe she has no husband?" whispered Mrs. O'Hara, a stout woman with a penchant for gossip and an aversion to personal boundaries.

"I hear she spends her evenings reading those French novels," replied Mrs. Thompson, clutching her pearls for dramatic effect.

"And did you see her hair? Not a single grey! Clearly unnatural," Mrs. O'Hara concluded, as if grey hair was a mandatory requirement for all respectable spinsters.

Stella, of course, heard every word. And why wouldn't she? The walls of her brownstone, though tall and sturdy, did little to keep out the chatter of Brooklyn's most dedicated rumor mill. Instead of retreating into the shadows, she decided to play the part they had written for her, albeit with a sardonic twist.

Her first act of defiance was enrolling her daughter, Sylvia, in the most prestigious school in the borough. It wasn't enough that Sylvia was the daughter of a woman with no husband. No, she had to be the best-educated daughter of a woman with no husband. This decision, naturally, caused quite a stir among the other mothers, who were both intrigued and horrified at the prospect of their children associating with the spawn of scandal.

"Oh, Sylvia, darling," cooed Mrs. Henderson, a mother of three perfectly ordinary children. "What does your mother do all day?"

Sylvia, inheriting her mother's sharp wit, replied with a straight face, "She counts her money and laughs at the absurdity of your expectations."

This response earned Sylvia a wide berth in the schoolyard but also a grudging respect from her peers. Stella couldn't have been prouder.

Stella's second act of rebellion was sending her own mother to a nursing home, a decision that was less about practicality and more about self-preservation. Her mother, a woman of formidable opinions and an endless supply of unsolicited advice, had become unbearable after her father Lucien's death.

"Stella, dear, you must find a new husband," her mother would say, shaking her head. "No man wants a woman who speaks her mind. It's simply not done."

"Mother," Stella would reply with an arched eyebrow, "if that's true, then I suppose I'm better off without one."

The nursing home was a luxurious establishment on the other side of town, far enough that her mother's critiques would be muted by distance but close enough to appease any lingering guilt. Stella visited her regularly, armed with fresh flowers and a steely resolve to keep the visits short.

"Stella, you look tired," her mother observed during one visit, her sharp eyes missing nothing. "You should get more rest."

"Mother, I'm raising a daughter, managing a household, and maintaining my sanity. Rest is a luxury I cannot afford," Stella replied, her smile tight.

Raising Sylvia alone in Brooklyn was a constant battle against societal norms. Invitations to social events were rare, and when they did come, they were often laced with pity rather than genuine camaraderie. Stella attended these events with her head held high, her laughter a bit too loud, and her comments a tad too sharp. She refused to be the quiet, demure widow society expected her to be.

At one particularly tedious tea party, Mrs. Goldstein, a woman whose wealth was matched only by her lack of tact, asked, "Stella, dear, don't you find it difficult managing everything on your own?"

Stella's smile was as sweet as arsenic. "Not at all, Mrs. Goldstein. In fact, it's rather liberating not having to answer to anyone but myself."

"You don't think that is selfish?" Mrs. Goldstein prodded Stella for common sense.

This remark, of course, was met with gasps and hurriedly averted eyes. Stella reveled in the discomfort, finding dark humor in the shocked expressions and whispered condemnations. She was, after all, living on her own terms in a world that demanded unity.

As the years passed, Stella's reputation in the neighborhood solidified. She was the woman who dared to live differently, who refused to be constrained by the narrow views of those around her. And while she faced many challenges, she did so with a resilience and a wit that left her neighbors both scandalized and secretly envious.

In her brownstone, amidst the whispers and the judgments, Stella found a strength she hadn't known she possessed. She was raising Sylvia to be strong, independent, and unapologetically herself. After all, as Stella often mused, life was too short to be lived by anyone else's rules.

With each turn of the page, Emma found herself unraveling from her family's somewhat extravagant and avant garde lives—a past filled with grandeur and scandal, but also resilience and the unyielding spirit of women who dared to defy convention. In the quiet solitude of her expansive library, Emma's thoughts wandered to Franz, her steadfast husband working as a heart surgeon. She wondered how he would react to the revelations buried within these pages—secrets that could reshape their understanding of the Bovary legacy. She was now Mrs. Franz Kettering, but deep down, she would always be a Bovary.

As the stories wore on, Emma felt a sense of empowerment wash over her. Berthe's bold choices and unwavering determination inspired Emma to embrace her own desires and aspirations fully. She closed the diary with a smile, knowing that her journey to France, to meet her paternal relatives and explore her heritage, was going to allow her to live authentically and see a side to herself she had only sketched in with flights of whimsy and girlhood hopes and dreams. If only she could convince Stella, her aging grandmother to fly with her.

She got out of her papasan with a scurry and placed the book back on the shelf. Its battered spine finding rest between Harry Potter and Colleen Hoover. Stretching, she contemplated whether or not she should divulge her Bovary history to Franz. It was a delicate choice, and she decided that she would keep it to herself.

The rest of her day was filled with the clatter of keyboards and the soft glow of screens, as she worked as a marketing executive, crafting narratives that sold dreams to others—tales of luxury, adventure, and aspiration. Yet, beneath the veneer of her meticulously curated life, Emma harbored a restlessness that whispered of unfulfilled desires.

Her friends, a glamorous gaggle of socialites, were married to old money and older husbands, and their lives seemed like a never-ending carousel of luxury and leisure. They would spend their weekends flitting from one exclusive event to another, their days filled with brunches at the Plaza, shopping sprees on Fifth Avenue, and evenings at private clubs where the champagne flowed like water.

Emma, by comparison, felt like an outsider in her own life. Yet, she couldn't help but be drawn into their world, even if it meant grappling with a toxic mix of envy and jealousy. She knew her mother had gone through the same trials and tribulations, and she was happy to visit with her soon. Stella would be thrilled about Emma's nuptials with Franz The Doughboy, as her grandmother lovingly referred to him.

Her husband, Franz, was a competent doctor with a heart as steady as his medical practice. He possessed a gentle demeanor and a steadfast devotion that had drawn Emma to him in the first place. Their stylish home, perched high above the bustling streets of Brooklyn, boasted panoramic views that shimmered with the promise of urban sophistication. Franz, with his predictable routines and earnest commitment to his patients, provided Emma with the stability she craved. Stella had left the brownstone to her as a graduation gift years ago when Stella herself had moved to SoHo to be a part of the fashion scene. She was still able to sell her mother's fashions to collectors and heiresses.

Yet, for Emma, security was not enough. Her days blurred together in a symphony of deadlines and client meetings, where she spun tales of escape and romance with a skill that belied her own yearning for a storybook love. She craved excitement, passion—moments that would ignite her spirit and infuse her life with the vibrant hues of an artist's palette. Emma often wondered if the universe had a twisted sense of humor, or if fate just had a penchant for irony. After all, how else could she explain her relationship with Franz, a man who could make watching paint dry seem like an action-packed thriller?

They met in the most unremarkable of circumstances: a health and wellness seminar hosted by her marketing firm. Emma was there to create a campaign for a new line of gluten-free, kale-infused snacks. Franz was there to speak about managing epilepsy with a balanced diet and stress reduction. His presentation was thorough and informative, delivered in a voice that could soothe even the most caffeinated insomniac into a stupor.

When Franz's seizure struck mid-presentation, Emma was the first to react. She found his vulnerability endearing and his subsequent recovery lecture on the nuances of epilepsy surprisingly captivating.

She offered him a ride home, which he accepted with a mild look of surprise. The Uber ride through Brooklyn's evening streets was filled with a curious mix of small talk and deeper confessions. By the time they reached his place, Franz had shyly asked for her number over a cup of coffee he quietly made for them.

"You know," Emma said, her fingers tracing the rim of her cup, "I am glad you didn't die up there. To be honest, I wouldn't kill you even if you asked."

Franz nodded thoughtfully. "My work as a doctor has shown me just how much suffering some patients endure. Sometimes, the humane thing to do is to let them go peacefully and protect their dignity."

Emma looked at him with a newfound curiosity. "Exactly. And with abortion, it's the same? We have a solemn duty to protect human life."

Franz leaned in, his blue eyes serious. "I've seen too many women in desperate situations because they didn't have access to safe abortions. It's not just a medical issue, it's a human rights issue."

Emma smiled, feeling a connection she hadn't anticipated. "I'm glad you see it that way. Too many people are so black and white about these things."

Franz chuckled. "Speaking of black and white, are you only a marketing executive, or do you have an OnlyFans account, too? I love a working woman." He felt stupid after he said this, and he looked down at his own cup.

Emma laughed. " Not at all. Well, someone's got to keep things interesting. Besides, it's not much different from DoorDash, really. Both are just services we use to get what we want, right? One delivers food, the other delivers... well I don't know.." She felt instantly comfortable with Franz, ready for him to make the next move.

Franz nearly spat out his coffee. "I'm not sure the DoorDash drivers would appreciate that comparison, but I see your point."

They continued to talk, delving into their beliefs and values with a frankness that was both surprising and exhilarating. By the time the evening ended, Emma felt a strange mix of relief and excitement. Here was a man who not only accepted her quirks and strong opinions but seemed to genuinely appreciate them.

As she began to leave, Franz turned to her with a shy smile. "Thank you for the ride, and for the conversation. It's not often I meet someone who's willing to talk about such heavy topics so openly."

Emma smiled back. "It's been a pleasure. And hey, if you're ever in need of a DoorDash delivery, you know who to call."

Franz laughed, his face lighting up. "I'll keep that in mind. Goodnight, Emma."

As she ordered her rideshare, Emma couldn't help but feel a strange sense of optimism. Maybe, just maybe, she had found someone who could handle her brand of dark humor and complex morality. Someone who, like her, believed in the importance of choice and the right to life.

Their courtship was nothing short of a series of lukewarm encounters. Dinners at quiet, dimly lit restaurants, where their conversations were punctuated by the sounds of forks scraping plates and the occasional awkward silence. Walks through Central Park that felt more like obligatory strolls through a nursing home garden than romantic outings. Emma found herself charmed by his gentle nature, even if it sometimes felt like she was dating a character from a medical journal.

Franz's epilepsy was a constant companion in their relationship, a third wheel that neither of them particularly minded. He would have the occasional seizure, and Emma would handle it with a calm efficiency that made her feel more like a nurse than a girlfriend. It wasn't glamorous, but it was their reality.

One evening, as they sat in Emma's living room, watching a documentary about the migration patterns of Canadian geese (Franz's choice, naturally), she suggested he move in with her. "It's just practical," she said, though she privately admitted to herself that his presence provided a peculiar kind of comfort. Franz agreed, and soon, he was ensconced in her ancestral Brooklyn brownstone, a place that reeked of old money and older ghosts.

Emma was a marketing executive with a knack for crafting compelling narratives, though she sometimes felt her own life lacked the excitement of the campaigns she created. Franz, with his encyclopedic knowledge of neurology and his mild-mannered charm, appreciated her creative streak, even if he didn't fully understand it. They saved a lot of money living together in the brownstone, a place that had seen better days but still held a certain stately charm.

They were currently planning their honeymoon to Puerto Rico, a destination chosen more for its affordability than its romantic appeal. Emma found herself in the newly renovated kitchen, a space that was more HGTV than History Channel, pouring herself a glass of water. The sleek granite countertops and stainless steel appliances stood in stark contrast to the dusty, antique furniture that filled the rest of the house. She stared out the window, contemplating the mundane reality of her life and the equally mundane future she was stepping into.

In the evening, as the city's lights flickered to life like stars against the urban backdrop, Emma found herself standing by the window of their chic abode waiting for Franz's shift to finally end. It was in fact their wedding night, and she knew he wouldn't be late. Thinking about her upcoming vacations, she sighed contentedly against the backdrop of traffic below, which seemed to mock the stillness that settled within her, stirring an ache for something more profound than the material comforts that surrounded her.

Franz, oblivious to the tempest brewing in his wife's heart, returned home with a bouquet of flowers and tales of his patients' recoveries and the latest medical breakthroughs. He was particularly passionate about anesthesia-free surgeries. Dragging, he listened intently as Emma recounted her day, her voice tinged with a wistfulness he attributed to her artistic temperament.

Emma stood in the kitchen, the glass of water cool in her hand as she watched Franz's calm demeanor. A mischievous thought crossed her mind, and she set the glass down. Without a word, she crossed the room to him, her steps soft on the polished wood floor.

"Franz," she murmured, her voice low and inviting. He looked up, his eyes meeting hers with a gentle curiosity. Before he could respond, she leaned in and pressed her lips to his, a sweet kiss that quickly deepened. Her hands found their way to his shoulders, and she felt him relax into her embrace, his arms wrapping around her waist.

He held her close, the familiar scent of antiseptic clinging to his skin from the long day at the hospital. She pulled back just enough to catch her breath, a playful smile on her lips. "Come with me," she whispered, taking his hand and leading him to the bathroom.

The bathroom, a mix of modern fixtures and antique charm, was bathed in the soft glow of the evening light. She turned on the shower, the steam rising as the water heated up. Franz watched her, his expression a blend of admiration and slight bewilderment. Emma reached for the buttons of his shirt, her fingers deftly undoing them one by one. He let out a small sigh of relief as she slid the shirt off his shoulders, the tension of the day melting away.

"Let's get you cleaned up," she said, her voice a husky murmur. She helped him out of his clothes, her hands lingering on his skin, tracing the lines of his muscles. Franz's breath hitched as she brushed her lips against his collarbone, her touch both tender and tantalizing.

They stepped into the shower together, the hot water cascading over them. Emma grabbed the soap, lathering it in her hands before running them over his chest, washing away the grime of the day. Her touch was firm yet gentle, her movements deliberate and intimate.

Franz closed his eyes, leaning into her touch, the sensation both soothing and electrifying.

She reached up, her fingers threading through his damp hair, massaging his scalp. He let out a low groan of pleasure, his hands finding their way to her waist, pulling her closer. The water streamed over them, the sound mingling with their soft gasps and murmurs. Emma's hands roamed over his body, each touch a promise of more to come.

When they finally stepped out of the shower, the air around them was thick with steam and anticipation. Emma grabbed a towel, drying him off with the same care and attention she had shown in the shower. She wrapped the towel around herself, her eyes never leaving his.

Their beige bedroom awaited, a sanctuary of soft linens and warm light. Franz followed her, his eyes dark with desire. Emma led him to the bed, her hands trailing over his skin, igniting a fire between them. She pushed him gently onto the bed, climbing on top of him, her movements slow and deliberate.

They came together with a fervor that sometimes surprised them both accounting for their usual reserved natures, their bodies moving in perfect harmony. The beige walls of the bedroom seemed to close in, creating a cocoon of intimacy around them. Franz's hands roamed over her body, exploring every curve and contour, his touch both reverent and hungry.

Emma's breath hitched as he whispered her name, his voice rough with emotion. She leaned down, capturing his lips in a kiss that was both sweet and searing. Their connection deepened, each touch and caress building towards a crescendo.

When they finally lay tangled in the sheets, their bodies spent and sated, Emma felt a sense of contentment wash over her. She looked at Franz, his eyes closed, a small smile playing on his lips. She reached out, brushing a damp lock of hair from his forehead.

"Franz," she whispered, her voice soft and filled with affection. He opened his eyes, meeting her gaze with a look of pure adoration.

"I love you," he said simply, his words a balm to her restless soul.

"I love you too," she replied, snuggling closer to him.

The next afternoon, while Franz attended a medical conference uptown, Emma found herself wandering through the streets of Brooklyn. She passed trendy cafes and boutique shops, where couples laughed over brunch and artists sketched their dreams onto canvases. Impulsively Emma strode into the Cafe D'Art store and purchased her own machinations.

At a corner bookstore, she stumbled upon a novel that seemed to beckon to her from the shelf—a story of passion, obsession, and the intoxicating allure of forbidden love. The words leapt off the page, weaving themselves into a supportive quilt of her thoughts with an urgency that seized her heart. She purchased the book, its cover a promise of escape from the mundane reality that threatened to suffocate her.

That evening, as the city's lights painted patterns on the walls of their apartment, Emma curled up on the sofa with the novel cradled in her hands. The protagonist's tumultuous affair unfolded before her eyes, igniting a firestorm of emotions that had long lain dormant within her. She read late into the night, the words echoing in her mind like a symphony of longing and desire.

As she was preparing her solo evening meal, she realized that Berthe and Stella were shielding her from something, someone. They wanted her life to be exactly the way it is now. She was here. She showed up. Now what? She wondered to herself as she chopped baby potatoes and fresh arugula.

She was lost in thought when Franz returned home, weary but content from his day, he looked adoringly at his wife. He brushed a skin of potato off of her cheek with his thumb, his heart heavy with a tenderness that bordered on apprehension. He knew then, in the quiet of their Brooklyn apartment, that Emma's restless spirit had begun to stir—and that their story was about to take an unexpected turn into uncharted territory, where the lines between reality and fiction blurred in the pursuit of an elusive, storybook romance. He was silently preparing his heart for the worst.

"I found this in the back of my mother's diary. I wasn't going to say anything, but this seemed too important." Emma reached out a manicured hand and placed the tattered note in Franz's.

Dear [Recipient],

As I write this letter, my heart weighs heavy with regret and sorrow. The dreams I once cherished, the passions that consumed me, they have all led me down a path of despair and ruin. I find myself at the end of my journey, alone and desolate.

I took the poison today, not out of impulse but out of a desperate longing for peace. The weight of my debts, the shame of my mistakes, and the betrayal of my own ideals have crushed me beyond repair. I have lived a life fueled by illusions, chasing after fleeting happiness that was never meant for me.

My dear [Recipient], forgive me for the pain I leave behind. I hope you can understand the depths of my despair and the futility of my struggles. I could not bear to face another day in this world of hypocrisy and false promises.

Please remember me not for my mistakes but for the dreams I once held dear. Know that I sought love and beauty, only to find emptiness and deceit. May you find solace where I could not, and may my story serve as a cautionary tale against the dangers of yearning for an unattainable ideal.

With love and regret,

Emma

Franz remained unfazed as he placed the note on the granite counter. He took his time to process what he had just read. Emma stared at him until he returned to her.

"Your... Let me get this straight. Your great-great-great-grandmother took poison and this is her suicide note?" Franz innocently inquired.

"Yes. My grandma Stella told me that Emma had killed herself when her daughter Berthe was just a child."

Emma Bovary sat in her Brooklyn brownstone, surrounded by the vintage charm she had grown tired of. She pondered what kind of father Franz would be- surely better than her own. Her own grandfather was a rich Frenchman who she saw only at NASCAR races every few years. He had plunged headfirst into the world of gambling and she never saw him peaceful again. Antonie was the world's greatest failure. She glanced at the old photograph on her mantelpiece — Berthe, her grandmother, with a distant look in her eyes, taken long before Emma was born.

As she sipped her tea in the quiet of her brownstone, Emma wondered about Berthe's life — the sacrifices, the dreams deferred, and the quiet resilience that seemed to run in their family. With a sigh, Emma put down her worries and drew a bath. It was 2024 afterall, she should not have to think in terms of the past when framing her future. Franz could tell Emma was onto something. When she got like this, he got out of her way. Emma eased herself into the tub. Letting the water roll down her shoulders, she thanked God for the decision to marry Franz.

In the tub, Emma reflected on her own parents. Her mother had a brief fling with a taxi driver in Brooklyn, but was killed shortly after. Stella, her grandmother, raised her into the strong and talented executive that she was. Emma held a shampoo bottle gently in her hand as she thought about what it would be like to have her own parents to care for her.

As she pieced together Berthe's narrative of resilience and sacrifice, Emma couldn't help but draw parallels to her own life. Married to Franz, a kind-hearted but predictable physician, Emma felt a yearning for more—a deeper connection, adventure, and a touch of the romanticism her ancestor had chased.

Emma's discovery of Berthe's history stirred something within her—a desire to reconnect with her French roots. She envisioned herself strolling through Parisian boulevards, exploring the grand estates of her aristocratic relatives, and perhaps uncovering family secrets hidden in dusty attics or forgotten journals. The allure of discovering a wealthy, distant branch of the Bovary family sparked her imagination.

She spent the rest of the evening regaling on past career triumphs to pump her up for the annual Brand-A-Thon, a marketing expo, she would be attending and contributing to in the morning. Getting out of the tub and drying off, she looked at herself tired in the steamy mirror. With a sigh, she went to her bed. She kissed her husband goodnight, and turned out the light.

Emma woke up with a jolt of excitement. Today was the day of the Brand-A-Thon, an event she had been eagerly anticipating. She sprang up, her mind already racing with the day's agenda. As she hurriedly got dressed, she couldn't help but feel a twinge of guilt for waking Franz so early. He mumbled a sleepy goodbye as she kissed him and rushed out the door.

With a spring in her step, Emma navigated the busy streets of Brooklyn, heading towards the Marriott where she was meeting her grandmother, Stella, for a quick brunch. Stella had always been a source of inspiration and fascination for Emma, with her perfectly manicured nails, flawless makeup, and a life full of enigmatic stories.

Emma entered the hotel's restaurant and immediately spotted Stella, sitting gracefully at a table with a glass of pineapple mimosa in hand. Her grandmother's elegant appearance always seemed to be perfectly timed, and today was no exception. Stella looked up, her face lighting up with a practiced smile.

"Emma, darling! Over here!" Stella waved her over.

Emma hurried to the table and sat down, her own excitement bubbling over. "Good morning, Grandma. You look amazing, as always. How is SoHo?"

Stella chuckled, her eyes sparkling with amusement. "Well, you know, a little Botox and a lot of self-care go a long way. How are you feeling about today?"

"I'm so excited! But also a bit nervous," Emma admitted. "I wanted to talk to you about something that's been bothering me."

Stella raised an impeccably groomed eyebrow. "Oh? Do tell."

Emma took a deep breath. "I've been feeling... envious lately. Of my friends with their glamorous lives and wealthy husbands. Sometimes, it feels like I'm not living my own life anymore, just watching theirs and wishing it were mine."

Stella's smile softened and she took a sip. Then, she leaned in closer. "Ah, envy and jealousy. Old friends of mine. Let me tell you a story. It was a typical Saturday morning when I found myself at a lavish brunch in one of her friend's Upper East Side penthouse. The room was filled with the scent of fresh lilies and the soft clinking of silverware on fine china. My friends, bedecked in designer dresses and dripping with jewels, were lounging on plush sofas, sipping mimosas and exchanging the latest gossip about art auctions and charity galas.

"Did you hear about the new gallery opening in Chelsea?" asked Clarissa, her friend with an ever-present air of ennui. "I heard they flew in a Banksy piece for the exhibit."

"Oh, I know," sighed Miranda, another friend who had perfected the art of looking perpetually bored. "Charles is on the board, so we got a private viewing last week. Simply divine."

Stella forced a smile, nodding along as if she were part of their rarified world. Inside, she seethed with a sense of inadequacy and frustration. Her friends' lives seemed like a series of gilded highlights, while hers felt like an endless loop of bills, deadlines, and solitude.

"Stella, darling, how's your little design business going?" Clarissa asked, her tone dripping with condescension.

"Oh, it's going well," Stella lied, her voice tight. "I just landed a new client."

"That's lovely," Miranda said, not really listening. "You know, I think it's so brave of you to work for yourself. I could never do it. Too much uncertainty."

Brave. The word felt like a dagger wrapped in velvet. Stella nodded again, taking a large gulp of her mimosa. She glanced around the room, taking in the opulence that surrounded her. The antique furniture, the crystal chandeliers, the priceless art on the walls. It was a world she could visit but never truly belong to, and the realization gnawed at her insides.

As the day wore on, they moved from brunch to a high-end spa, where they lounged in fluffy robes and indulged in treatments that cost more than Stella's monthly electric bill. She listened to their idle chatter about their husbands' business ventures, their children's boarding schools, and their upcoming vacations to exotic locales. Each word was like a needle, pricking at her sense of self-worth.

By the time they were sipping cocktails at a rooftop bar with panoramic views of the city, Stella felt like a hollow shell. Her friends laughed and toasted to their perfect lives, oblivious to the storm brewing inside her.

"Cheers to us!" Clarissa exclaimed, raising her glass. "And to our fabulous lives!"

Stella raised her glass mechanically, her smile frozen in place. Inside, she was screaming. She envied their wealth, their status, their seemingly effortless happiness. The comparison to her own life was unbearable, and it filled her with a deep, aching sense of despair.

That night, as she lay in her beautifully decorated brownstone, Stella thanked God for her safety, her home, her family, and her good decisions. She couldn't shake the feeling that she was living a life half-lived, a shadow of the existence she had always dreamed of. She stared at the ceiling, the weight of her envy pressing down on her like a physical force.

"I began working on myself. I saw a therapist and worked through many of my own insecurities. Soon after I met Antonie, and I had your mother. My life became so busy that I didn't have time to think about anyone else. Mother's seamstress business was picking up, and the ladies I spent time with all had her fashions on. Some of them were unaware who crafted their garb, but I knew. Deep down, it gave me a sense of belonging. Nowadays, though, you just see fast-fashion everywhere." Stella, looking resigned, used her hand to gesture 'nevermind,' as if casting off an entire lifetime of hard work and toil by her mother.

After a half an hour, Emma got up, kissed her grandmother goodbye, and made her way to the marketing expo. Her heart fluttered with excitement and nerves. As the director at a large corporation, she had been selected as a keynote speaker, a prestigious opportunity that she had worked tirelessly to earn.

She checked her phone: a message from Franz. "Good luck today! Love you!" She rolled her eyes. Was it possible to be allergic to niceness?

As she made her way through the Expo, her thoughts took on a darkly humorous tone. She pictured herself in one of those vintage sitcoms, with a laugh track following her every move. "And here we have Emma Bovary, Marketing Maven Extraordinaire, suffering from an acute case of domestic dullness."

The expo hall buzzed with energy. Stalls and booths were set up with vibrant displays, each vying for attention. Emma navigated the crowd, her mind focused on the speech she had meticulously prepared. She approached the stage, where her name was prominently displayed on a banner: Emma Bovary, Director of Strategic Marketing, Bell Corp.

Just then, a handsome man appeared, as if conjured by her discontent. He introduced himself as Leon, and his charm was palpable. They exchanged pleasantries, but his eyes held a promise of something more.

"I've been looking forward to your talk," Leon said, leaning in slightly. "I'm sure it's going to be inspiring."

Emma couldn't help but laugh internally. Inspiring? She barely inspired herself to get out of bed some mornings. But there was something about Leon's intensity that sparked a flicker of excitement in her.

Emma shook his hand, feeling a slight blush creep up her cheeks. "Thank you.. That's very kind of you." Leon leaned in a little closer, his eyes twinkling with interest. "I've been looking forward to your talk. I'm sure it's going to be inspiring."

Emma smiled, trying to maintain her composure. "I hope so. It's a topic I'm very passionate about." Before she could say more, the event coordinator signaled that it was time for her to begin. Emma gave Leon a polite nod and ascended the steps to the stage. As she adjusted the microphone, she glanced back to see Leon watching her intently from the audience. Emma stood at the edge of the stage, adjusting the microphone and glancing out at the sea of faces. The air in the conference hall was thick with anticipation, the kind that usually accompanied product launches or the announcement of a new iPhone model. Today, it was all about Data-Driven Marketing, and Emma was the star attraction.

Her stomach fluttered with nerves, not just because of the speech, but because she had spotted him—Leon—sitting in the front row, looking effortlessly handsome and impossibly interested in everything she had to say. She took a deep breath and began.

"Ladies and gentlemen, esteemed colleagues, and data enthusiasts," Emma started, her voice steady despite the inner turmoil. "Today, we're diving into the world of data-driven marketing, where numbers tell stories and algorithms whisper sweet nothings into our ears. But first, a confession: I once thought data was as dry as a well-done steak. Now, I see it as the filet mignon of marketing—juicy, tender, and impossible to ignore."

A ripple of laughter passed through the audience. Good, she thought, keep it light. Keep them engaged.

"You see, in our quest to understand our customers, we've come to rely on data more than ever. Gone are the days when marketing was about gut feelings and guesswork. Now, we can pinpoint exactly what our customers want, sometimes before they even know it themselves. It's a bit like playing God, but with fewer plagues and more targeted ads."

She glanced at Leon, who was nodding appreciatively, a slight smile playing on his lips. Focus, Emma, focus.

"Imagine, if you will, a world where your favorite restaurant knows you're craving pizza before you do. You might think it's a miracle, or you might think it's creepy. Either way, it's the power of data. And speaking of miracles and slightly creepy things, let's talk about predictive analytics."

The crowd chuckled again, and Emma felt a surge of confidence. "Predictive analytics is like having a crystal ball, but one that actually works. It allows us to anticipate customer behavior, making our campaigns more effective and our results more predictable. It's the closest thing to magic we have, without needing a wand or risking a hex."

She paused, taking a sip of water. "Now, I know what you're thinking. 'Emma, isn't there a dark side to all this data?' Absolutely. There's always a dark side. But it's our job to use this power responsibly, to balance personalization with privacy. After all, we don't want to end up in a dystopian future where our fridges judge us for that midnight ice cream binge."

The room erupted in laughter, and Emma stole another glance at Leon. His eyes were fixed on her, sparkling with amusement and something else she couldn't quite place.

"To wrap up, data-driven marketing is about more than just numbers. It's about creating connections, understanding our customers on a deeper level, and delivering experiences that resonate. It's not just about selling products; it's about telling stories, stories that our customers want to hear and be a part of."

She took a deep breath, ready to conclude. "In the end, data-driven marketing is like a good romance novel—full of twists and turns, unexpected insights, and a happy ending. And if we're lucky, maybe a bit of passion, too."

The audience applauded, and Emma felt a rush of exhilaration. As she stepped off the stage, Leon was there, waiting for her. "Great speech," he said, his voice warm and genuine. "You really brought the data to life."

"Thanks." She replied, her heart racing for reasons entirely unrelated to data. "I just hope I didn't scare anyone off with the dystopian fridge." Her jesting to herself almost knocked her off course and into the waiting arms of this mystery man. Catching all remaining fragments of self-respect, she hunkered down and resolved herself to stay on track.

"Not at all," he laughed. "In fact, I think you might have inspired a few people to check their privacy settings."

They shared a smile, and in that moment, Emma felt a spark of something new and exciting. It wasn't just about data anymore. It was about possibilities—both professional and personal.

As they walked out together, heading towards the post-conference luncheon, Emma couldn't help but feel a twinge of guilt. She was supposed to be planning a honeymoon to Puerto Rico with Franz. But here she was, with Leon, feeling more alive than she had in years.

He smiled, a playful glint in his eyes. "Maybe we could grab a coffee later and discuss your ideas in more detail? I'd love to hear more about your perspective on marketing strategies."

Emma hesitated for a moment, the thrill of the day still coursing through her veins. "That sounds great." She said professionally.

Feeling the challenge, Leon handed her his business card. "Call me when you're free."

Emma took the card, slipping it into her purse. As she watched Leon walk away, she felt a sense of excitement that she hadn't felt in a long time. She could not deny a magnetic pull to him, and perhaps this day would be more interesting than she had anticipated.

Turning back to the bustling expo, she felt a renewed sense of purpose. Today was just the beginning. And as she moved through the crowd, she couldn't help but feel that her grandmother's advice had been spot on. Living authentically and embracing the unexpected moments was truly the key to happiness.

After her talk, which went swimmingly, Leon approached her again. They exchanged numbers, and he suggested they grab a coffee later. Emma agreed, feeling a thrill she hadn't felt in years. As she prepared for her coffee date with Leon, she mused about the absurdity of it all. Caring for Franz had become more of a chore than a joy. She was tired of playing the perfect wife, tired of their bland routines. Her mind wandered to Paris—a city synonymous with passion, adventure, and everything her life was not.

By the time she met Leon for coffee, she had already made up her mind. Puerto Rico? Forget it. Paris was where she needed to be, where she would truly come alive. She couldn't pinpoint why exactly, but she was curious enough to want to find out.

Emma Bovary walked into the quaint café, the air thick with the aroma of freshly brewed coffee and the murmurs of hushed conversations. The place had an old-world charm, a stark contrast to the sleek, modern marketing world she navigated daily. She spotted

Leon at a corner table, looking like he belonged on a magazine cover rather than a marketing convention. He stood up as she approached, flashing her a smile that could melt the iciest of hearts.

"Emma, over here!" Leon waved, his enthusiasm infectious. She smiled back, feeling a flutter in her stomach. It was purely professional, she reminded herself, just a friendly coffee meeting.

As she sat down, Leon ordered their drinks—a latte for her, an Americano for him. They exchanged pleasantries, discussing the usual industry gossip, the latest marketing trends, and the absurdity of some client requests. The conversation flowed effortlessly, and soon they were laughing like old friends.

"So," Leon leaned in, his eyes twinkling with curiosity, "what are your plans for the upcoming holiday?"

Emma hesitated for a moment. "I actually have a vacation planned for Paris. I thought it would be nice to take my grandmother. She is from there, and it's a city I've always wanted to explore more."

Leon raised an eyebrow, a sly smile creeping across his face. "Paris, you say? Coincidentally, there's a marketing convention happening there next month. What do you say we make it a business trip? We could attend the convention during the day and explore the city in the evenings."

Emma's mind raced. The idea of mixing business with pleasure, especially with Leon, was enticing. She thought about the dull routine she shared with Franz, his epilepsy adding a layer of predictability and responsibility that weighed her down. The spark she felt around Leon was a stark contrast, a breath of fresh air in her otherwise stifling life.

"That sounds... interesting," Emma replied, trying to sound nonchalant. "But I planned to take my grandmother. It's sort of a promise I made to her."

Leon nodded thoughtfully. "Why not bring her along? Paris is a city for everyone. We could still enjoy the convention and make it a memorable trip for her, too."

Emma mulled it over. The idea was becoming more appealing by the second. She imagined strolling along the Seine with Leon, attending the convention and then slipping away for romantic dinners. The thought of Paris, with its promise of adventure and escape, was irresistible.

"Alright," she said, a smile spreading across her face. "Let's do it. I'll bring my grandmother, and we'll turn it into a grand adventure."

Leon beamed. "Perfect. You won't regret it, Emma. Paris is going to be amazing."

After finishing their coffee, Emma returned home, her mind buzzing with excitement. She couldn't stop replaying her conversation with Leon in her head, imagining the possibilities that Paris held. Her heart raced as she thought about the secret thrill of the trip, the chance to break free from her mundane routine with Franz, and the ability to connect with her roots.

She sat down at her laptop, her fingers trembling slightly as she navigated the airline website. With each keystroke, the reality of the trip began to take shape. The thought of a Parisian adventure with Leon, of exploring the city's romantic streets and attending a glamorous marketing convention, filled her with a sense of boldness she hadn't felt in years. It was daring and a little reckless—everything she craved but rarely allowed herself to indulge in.

As she finalized the booking, a wave of exhilaration washed over her. She had just taken a step towards something new and exciting, something far removed from the predictable life she led with Franz. It was a decision driven by desire and a yearning for more, and it made her feel alive.

Emma picked up her phone and called her grandmother, Stella. Her voice wavered slightly as she spoke, trying to keep the giddiness in check. "Stella, I have some exciting news. I'm going to Paris next month for a business trip. I want you to come with me."

There was a pause on the other end of the line, long enough for Emma to worry that her grandmother would refuse. But then Stella's voice came through, filled with cautious enthusiasm. "Paris? Emma, that sounds wonderful, but are you sure it's just business?"

Emma laughed, though the sound was a bit too forced to be entirely convincing. "Of course, it's a marketing convention. But we'll have plenty of time to explore the city together. It will be a trip to remember."

Stella sighed, and Emma could almost hear the wheels turning in her mind. "I understand. It's just that I was hoping for some time just the two of us. But if it's for work, I suppose it's fine."

The disappointment in Stella's voice tugged at Emma's heart. She knew her grandmother was looking forward to a different kind of trip, one filled with quiet moments and heartfelt conversations. But Emma's longing for excitement and her secret plans with Leon overshadowed her guilt.

"We'll make it special, I promise," Emma said, injecting as much sincerity as she could muster into her voice. "Paris will be magical. Just think of all the places we can visit together—the Eiffel Tower, the Louvre, charming little cafés. It will be a mix of business and pleasure."

Stella's voice softened. "Alright, Emma. If you're sure. I'll start packing."

As Emma hung up the phone, a mixture of excitement and trepidation filled her. She was standing on the brink of something monumental, a journey that could change everything. The days leading up to the trip passed in a blur, each one filled with preparations and mounting anticipation. She threw herself into her work, all the while fantasizing about Paris with Leon.

Emma and Franz had been trying for a baby for the past few months. Each attempt was filled with hope, followed by a mix of anxiety and anticipation. Emma felt an intense momentum in her life, as if everything was accelerating towards a significant change. The idea of bringing a new life into the world both thrilled and terrified her. She felt unstoppable, as if the universe was aligning to give her everything she desired.

One evening, just before her trip to Paris, Emma and Franz made love with a fervor they hadn't felt in a long time. The act was tender, filled with whispered promises and lingering touches. Afterward, they lay together, tangled in the sheets, sharing dreams of their potential future family. Emma felt a deep connection with Franz, a warmth that made her heart ache with both love and guilt for the secrets she was keeping.

The morning of her departure arrived, and Emma was a whirlwind of activity. She packed her suitcase with precision, carefully selecting outfits that would impress at the marketing convention and charm during her off-hours in the City of Light. She kissed Franz goodbye with a heartfelt sincerity that left him smiling, unaware of the turmoil inside her. "I love you," she whispered, and he echoed the sentiment, pressing a soft kiss to her forehead.

Stella arrived at the brownstone, her suitcase an exquisite piece of designer luggage, gleaming with polished gold accents and monogrammed initials that screamed luxury. Her eyes sparkled with anticipation, a subtle yet unmistakable hint of vanity in her demeanor.

Emma greeted her grandmother warmly, enveloping Stella in a tight embrace that conveyed both love and respect. As they prepared to depart for the airport, Emma felt a surge of affection and gratitude towards Stella, who had always been a pillar of support and sophistication in her life.

Together, they navigated the bustling streets of Brooklyn, Stella's steps exuding an air of effortless elegance as if every pavement was a runway. The anticipation for their journey grew with each passing moment, blending Emma's excitement for Paris with Stella's unabashed love for indulgence and extravagance. As they boarded the plane, Emma's heart raced. She glanced at Stella, who was settling into her seat with a contented smile. Emma felt a pang of guilt for the deception, but she quickly pushed it aside. This trip was as much for Stella as it was for her. Paris would be an adventure for both of them, a blend of business and personal discovery.

The flight was smooth, the hours passing in a haze of in-flight movies, light conversation, and occasional naps. Emma found herself daydreaming about Paris, about the marketing convention, and about Leon. She wondered what it would be like to see him again, to share meals and strolls through the city, to explore the possibilities that lay ahead. The world needed doers, decision makers, and visionaries. Emma was going to map it out and make it happen.

When the plane finally touched down at Charles de Gaulle Airport, Emma felt a rush of excitement. She and Stella navigated the bustling terminal, collected their luggage, and made their way to their hotel. The streets of Paris were alive with the sounds of traffic, the chatter of pedestrians, and the scent of fresh pastries wafting from nearby bakeries.

Their hotel was a charming boutique establishment with wrought-iron balconies and a cozy, elegant lobby. After checking in and freshening up, Emma and Stella prepared to meet Leon for dinner. Emma chose a chic yet understated red dress, hoping to strike the right balance between professional and alluring. She applied a touch of makeup, her hands steady despite the butterflies in her stomach.

Emma stood in front of the mirror, adjusting the straps of her sleek, red satin dress. The low neckline and form-fitting silhouette accentuated her curves, giving her a confidence she rarely felt. Her dark hair fell in loose waves around her shoulders, framing her face with a touch of mystery. She applied a bold red lipstick, completing the look with a flourish.

Next to her, Stella twirled in front of another mirror, adjusting the elegant Parisian hat perched atop her silver hair. The pencil dress she wore was a classic black, tailored to perfection. Stella's years of refined taste and grace were evident in every gesture and movement.

Downstairs, Leon waited at the door of their hotel suite. Tall and stylishly dressed in a tailored suit, he exuded youthful energy and charm. His smile widened as he caught sight of Emma and Stella descending the stairs. His artistic flair was subdued by his regal appearance. *A prince no doubt*, Emma mused.

"Emma, Stella, welcome!" Leon greeted them warmly, stepping forward to kiss Stella on both cheeks in the traditional French manner. His eyes lingered on Emma as he greeted her, a subtle admiration in his gaze that didn't go unnoticed.

"Bonjour. It's wonderful to see you both," Leon said with genuine enthusiasm, his voice tinged with the melodic cadence of French. He gestured towards the pruned rose bushes and the surroundings of the restaurant, a haven of plush velvet and soft candlelight. "Shall we?" The restaurant was a haven of sophistication, with soft lighting and comfortable chairs. They settled into a corner table, the ambiance around them adding to the sense of occasion.

Leon, with his youthful exuberance and charisma, regaled them with tales of Parisian life that sparkled with charm and vivid detail. He spoke of hidden cafes tucked away in cobblestone alleys, of art galleries that whispered secrets of centuries past, and of evenings spent strolling along the Seine as the city's lights danced on the water.

Emma found herself leaning in, hanging on every word as Leon painted a picture of a city alive with history and romance. His anecdotes were peppered with humor and insight, drawing her deeper into the allure of Paris. Across the table, Stella listened with a fond smile, occasionally interjecting her own experiences from decades ago. She reminisced about Paris in her youth, describing the bustling boulevards and the grandeur of the Louvre through the eyes of a young woman captivated by the city's artistic soul.

As the evening unfolded in the elegant Parisian restaurant, Emma couldn't help but be intrigued by Stella's mysterious past in Paris, especially her relationship with Antonie. Over glasses of rich Bordeaux wine and the flickering candlelight, Emma leaned forward with curiosity.

"Stella, tell us about Paris in your younger days," Emma prompted, her eyes sparkling with anticipation.

Stella smiled knowingly, her Parisian hat casting a shadow over her eyes. "Ah, Paris," she began wistfully, her voice tinged with nostalgia. "It was a different time, my dears. Antonie was a dashing young banker with a penchant for adventure."

Leon leaned in, captivated. "An adventurer? How romantic!"

Stella chuckled softly. "Indeed, he fancied himself quite the romantic. We used to stroll along the Seine under the moonlight, Antonie reciting poems he wrote just for me."

Emma's imagination soared as Stella painted vivid scenes of clandestine meetings in Montmartre cafes and moonlit walks through the Jardin des Tuileries. Each tale seemed to transport them deeper into the heart of Paris's bohemian past.

"Did you ever visit the Louvre together?" Leon asked, his eyes bright with curiosity.

Stella nodded, a glint of mischief in her eyes. "Oh yes, but not always to admire the art," she teased, evoking laughter from Emma and Leon.

Their conversation flowed effortlessly, blending Leon's youthful enthusiasm with Stella's seasoned wisdom. Emma recounted a humorous mishap she had while attempting to order a traditional French dish, only to end up with something entirely unexpected due to her flawed pronunciation. "I thought I was asking for 'poisson' (fish)," she chuckled, "but apparently, my accent turned it into 'poison'! The waiter's expression was priceless."

Stella, with her years of worldly experience, added to the merriment with tales of cultural misunderstandings from her youth. "I once tried to compliment a Parisian woman on her hat," she recalled, "but my French failed me, and I accidentally insulted her hairstyle instead! Antonie had to smooth things over with his poetic charm."

Leon, ever the gracious host and storyteller, regaled them with a story of his own, involving a comical attempt to navigate the Paris metro system during a rush hour. "I ended up on the wrong train and ended up in a neighborhood I'd never heard of," he admitted, shaking his head with mock embarrassment. "But it turned into an adventure I'll never forget."

Their laughter echoed through the cozy corner of the restaurant, mingling with the soft music and the gentle clink of glasses. Each story added a vibrant thread to the tapestry of their evening together, creating a warm and unforgettable atmosphere in the heart of Paris. In that moment, amidst the glow of candlelight and the aroma of fine cuisine, they forged a bond that transcended time and place.

As they perused the menu, sampling exquisite French wines and savoring delicate dishes, Emma couldn't help but feel a newfound excitement bubbling within her. Leon's presence was magnetic, and Paris seemed to unfold before her like a dream waiting to be explored. She knew she needed to reel in Leon to see exactly what he was hoping to accomplish with her and the Bell Corp.

Throughout the evening, Emma's initial nerves melted away, replaced by a sense of exhilaration. She laughed freely at Leon's jokes, enjoying his company more than she had expected. Stella, observing the dynamics between them, played the role of the wise observer, silently noting the chemistry brewing between Emma and their charming guide.

Emma leaned forward slightly, intrigued by Leon's lively conversation and the genuine interest he showed in her plans for the upcoming convention. His enthusiasm was infectious, and she found herself laughing at his witty anecdotes about past marketing expos.

"So, Emma," Leon said with a playful grin, "what's your game plan for the convention? Any groundbreaking strategies up your sleeve?" His mouth was simply luscious as he spoke, and both Bovary women had to check themselves. Stella smiled, Emma was practically drooling.

Emma chuckled, a twinkle of excitement in her eyes. "Well, you know how it goes in the marketing world," she replied with a hint of mystery. "Always trying to stay one step ahead of the competition."

Leon raised an eyebrow playfully. "Ah, competition, huh? Speaking of which," he continued, leaning in closer, "what about Peach Inc.? They're your main rivals, right?"

Emma paused, momentarily caught off guard by his directness. She composed herself quickly, a smile playing on her lips. "Oh, Peach Inc.," she replied vaguely, careful not to reveal too much. "Yes, they're quite formidable."

Stella, sitting beside Emma, observed the exchange with amusement, her eyes twinkling knowingly. She gave Emma an encouraging nod, silently urging her to keep the conversation flowing.

Leon leaned back, taking a sip of his wine. "Well, here's to friendly competition," he said cheerfully, raising his glass. "May the best marketer win." He gave her a sly smile, one she hardly noticed at all. Feeling full, Emma sat back and placed her napkin on the table.

He saw this, and quickly decided to mirror her. Against his deeper desires, he kept the conversation light and airy.

"Paris at night is absolutely stunning. I am sure Stella knows its intrigue. Would you mind me showing you around after this?" Leon asked almost innocently.

Emma's eyes dropped to her empty plate. She looked up at Stella and then replied. "I am excited to experience it. Stella and I need some rest and relaxation and we have plenty of time for that." She nodded toward Leon.

He sensed her unease and politely agreed. Sitting back in his chair, he snapped his fingers to get the waiter's attention. In a quiet fury, the waiter came over and gave Leon the bill. Leon, smiling at the women, took the lead and put down his AmEx card. The women looked at him gratefully, and he was pleased with his prowess. It is not everyday you get the upper-class American women to fly out to Paris to meet you, afterall, he thought.

Emma, feeling deeply attracted to him, stood up and made a beeline for the door. Stella and Leon were debris left in her wake, and they humbly followed her every graceful move. Leon looked at Stella and grinned. Stella noticed and admired his catlike reflexes, and decided to stay sharp for Emma's sake. She knew the consequences of falling for the wrong man intimately. Feeling a bit indignant, she sighed and followed her party out into the warm night air.

Outside, letting the warm Parisian night into their bones, the party awkwardly stood in a circle. "Are you sure I cannot interest you in a nightcap or evening stroll?" Leon said in his most gentlemanly voice. Emma let out a soft laugh, and declined his invitation. Looking sheepish and at her disposal, Emma politely told him she would see him at the convention.

"Bon." He said optimistically.

Stella, ever the ombudsman and political navigator, steered Emma towards the hotel. She practically pushed Emma in the right direction, trying hard not to be noticed. Emma grinned, and then allowed Stella to walk her to the hotel room. As Emma looked over her shoulder at Leon, he smiled at her as he walked away.

"What was that?" Stella complained when they got upstairs to their lavish retreat.

Emma flopped onto the plush bed, her mind still buzzing from the charming evening with Leon.

"Can you believe how handsome he is?" Emma sighed, kicking off her heels. "And so witty too. Did you see the way he effortlessly captivated the entire room?"

Stella, perched elegantly in an armchair, adjusted her Parisian hat thoughtfully. "Indeed, my dear. He certainly knows how to hold one's attention." She paused, her eyes glinting mischievously. "You know, tomorrow morning, we should take a stroll to Yonville. It's a charming village not far from here. I used to visit with Antonie."

Emma perked up at the suggestion. "Yonville? That sounds lovely! What's it like?"

Stella smiled nostalgically. "Oh, darling, it's picturesque—cobblestone streets lined with quaint shops, a cozy café where the locals gather. Berthe didn't get a chance to visit, but after World War Two it was quite different. I think you'll find it quite enchanting."

Emma's imagination sparked with visions of exploring the quaint village with her grandmother. "Let's do it, Stella. Tomorrow morning, Yonville it is!"

Stella knelt beside her bed, whispering a prayer under her breath. "Please, Lord, let Emma stay focused. Paris is not the kind of place a senior should be on her own." She glanced at the clock, which read 11:47 PM. The city of lights was just getting started, and so, she feared, was Emma.

From the adjoining bathroom, Emma's voice sang out cheerfully, "Stella, do you think we should try the chocolate croissants again tomorrow? Or maybe the pain au chocolat?"

Stella sighed, a mix of exasperation and fondness. "Emma, we had three croissants today. I think our hearts can only handle so much buttery goodness."

Emma emerged from the bathroom, her face freshly scrubbed and her hair wrapped in a towel. "Nonsense! We're in Paris! We should live a little." She wiggled her eyebrows mischievously, then burst into laughter.

"Live a little," Stella muttered. "That's what I'm worried about." She rose from her knees and walked over to her suitcase. "Here," she said, tossing a pair of matching striped pajama sets to Emma. "I thought these would be cute."

Emma's eyes sparkled. "Adorable!"

They changed into their pajamas and slipped under the crisp white sheets of their suite, the Eiffel Tower twinkling in the distance like a beacon of adventure. Stella looked out of the window. *Not a sight Grandma Emma would have seen*, she thought to herself. The bed creaked as they settled in, the sounds of the Parisian streets filtering through the open window.

Stella turned to Emma, a serious look on her face. "Promise me you won't wander off tomorrow. We need to stick together."

Emma rolled her eyes playfully. "Relax, Stella. I've got this under control. I'm not going to wander off like some lost tourist."

"You are a lost tourist," Stella retorted, but she couldn't help but smile. Emma's enthusiasm was infectious, even if it did give her anxiety.

Emma propped herself up on one elbow, looking mischievous. "You know I am here for you, right?"

Stella groaned. "Enough already."

Emma made a cross over her heart. "Promise. Now, let's get some sleep. Tomorrow, we take Paris by storm!"

They giggled like schoolgirls until their laughter faded into the soft sounds of sleep. Stella lay awake for a moment longer, her mind racing with worry and anticipation. She prayed silently once more, hoping that tomorrow would be filled with nothing but harmless adventures and perhaps a few more chocolate croissants.

It was interesting that Emma met a man named Leon who was also French. It was almost creepy knowing that Emma also married a doctor.

If she knew the similarities between herself and her mother, would she be happier? Stella thought to herself.

Just as she drifted off, a thought crossed her mind. "If Emma gets herself into trouble, I swear I'll—"

Her thought was cut short by a loud snore from Emma, who had already fallen into a deep, untroubled sleep. Stella shook her head, smiling despite herself. "Goodnight, Emma," she whispered, finally allowing herself to relax. "Here's to my baby learning the truth." She said with the silent resolution her mother had taught her.

Part 2

In the belly of a plane, she sits, shoulders bare, her heart's heritage, Madame Bovary's dare. In search of love and scandal deep, to Paris she flies, in dreams she'll sleep. Secrets swirl where none can blame, a silent heir to a throne built on shame.

Her ancestors' whispers haunt the air, of passion's grip and affairs unfair. Emma's bold requiem cannot go unnoticed, for in the silence the truths wings do flutter. With suitcase packed and heart on fire, she ventures forth, to unearth her clutter.

In quaint cafes where poets write, she sips her wine by candlelight. It is true that she is the maiden that legends were made of. Perhaps the mere product of a musing fling, but deep down a siren's queen. In a quest to be dominated by a spirit pure and true, she flies to the origin where love was new.

With each macaron and Parisian kiss, she learns the truth of love amiss.

Oh, Emma, descendant of bold Bovary, your journey's end, a past beginning with love's first kiss.

The first light of dawn crept through the thin lace curtains, casting a gentle glow over the hotel room. Stella stirred, her eyes fluttering open. She blinked a few times, trying to orient herself. For a moment, she forgot she was in Paris, the memories of the night before swirling like mist in her mind. Then, as the events came back to her, she sighed deeply and slipped out of bed.

Emma was still fast asleep, her soft snores filling the room. Stella smiled at the sight of her granddaughter, who looked peaceful and carefree. She moved quietly, not wanting to disturb Emma, and headed to the bathroom.

As she splashed cold water on her face, Stella couldn't help but think about the trip they were taking today—to Yonville. The last time she had visited the quaint town was in the 1970s, during one of the most tumultuous periods of her life. She closed her eyes for a moment, recalling the passion and heartbreak that had defined her affair with Antoine. They had met in Boston, yet their trist had taken her halfway around the world, and what started as an innocent flirtation quickly escalated into a whirlwind romance.

Antoine had been everything—adventurous, spontaneous, and utterly intoxicating. They had stolen moments together, escaping to the countryside whenever they could. Yonville had been their secret haven, a place where they could be free from the prying eyes of the city.

Stella shook her head, trying to dispel the memories. It had been over fifty years, and so much had changed since then. She was no longer that young, reckless woman. She had grown older, hopefully wiser, and had come to terms with the choices she had made. Antonie was long gone by now, a harsh truth she faced daily. Without him, though, Emma would not be here with her today.

She dressed quickly, choosing only the most sophisticated attire for the day's journey. As she brushed her hair, she caught her reflection in the mirror. The lines on her face told the story of a life well-lived, with all its joys and sorrows. She wondered what she would find in Yonville. Would it be the same charming village she remembered, or had time changed it beyond recognition?

Emma stirred in her sleep, muttering something unintelligible. Stella glanced at her beloved granddaughter, grateful for her companionship. Emma had been a constant in her life, through all the ups and downs. She made a mental note to thank her for insisting on this trip. It felt good to reconnect with her past, even if it was a little painful.

The clock ticked softly, reminding Stella that it was almost time to wake Emma. She closed her journal and stood, taking a deep breath. Today was a new day, and she was determined to face it with an open heart and mind. She walked over to Emma's bed and gently shook her shoulder. "Emma, it's time to get up. We've got a train to catch."

Emma groaned, burying her face in the pillow. "Five more minutes," she mumbled.

Stella chuckled. "Come on, sleepyhead. We don't want to miss our train."

Reluctantly, Emma sat up, rubbing her eyes. "Fine, fine. I'm up." She stretched and yawned, then gave Stella a curious look. "You're up early. Everything okay?"

Stella nodded, a small smile playing on her lips. "Just thinking about Yonville. It's been a long time."

Emma's expression softened. "It'll be good for you, Stella. A chance to see how things have changed, and maybe even find some closure."

"Rise and shine, my dear," Stella chirped, her voice annoyingly chipper for such an early hour. "We have a busy day ahead of us, and we must look our absolute best."

Emma sat up, rubbing her eyes and trying to shake off the remnants of her dreams. She glanced over at Stella, who was dressed in an elegant yet casual outfit that somehow screamed Parisian royalty. A soft, cream-colored blouse tucked into high-waisted navy trousers, complete with a chic beret tilted just so. She looked like she had stepped straight out of a 1950s French film.

"You look like you're ready to meet the Queen," Emma remarked dryly, her voice still thick with sleep.

"Not the Queen, darling. Just the best of Paris. Now hurry up and get dressed. We have places to be."

Emma rolled out of bed and began rifling through her suitcase, pulling out a pair of perfectly tailored jeans and a simple but stylish black top. She paired it with a light trench coat and a pair of classic ballet flats. Casual but elegant—just what Stella would approve of. After a quick run-through with her hairbrush and a dash of lipstick, she felt somewhat ready to face the day.

As they headed down to breakfast, Emma turned to Stella. "So, why exactly are we going to Yonville? I thought we were here for the convention."

Stella gave her a knowing smile, her eyes twinkling with mischief. "Ah, Yonville. A place steeped in history, my dear. And not just any history—our history. It's time you learned about your heritage."

Emma sighed, sipping her coffee. "You mean our scandalous ancestor, Madame Bovary. This isn't just a sentimental journey, is it?"

Stella chuckled, her laughter echoing lightly in the elegant dining room. "Oh, Emma, sometimes I think you're just like me. Yes, we're here for the convention, but we must seize the opportunity to explore our roots. Besides, a little scandal never hurt anyone."

Emma raised an eyebrow. "Isn't that the plot of every tragic novel ever written?"

"Precisely!" Stella replied with a flourish. "Now, finish your croissant. We've got history to make."

As they made their way to the station, Emma couldn't help but feel a mix of excitement and dread. She was used to Stella's whims, but this trip felt different. More personal, more revealing. They boarded the train to Yonville, the countryside speeding past them as Stella began recounting stories of their infamous ancestor.

"You see, Emma, Madame Bovary was a woman ahead of her time. Passionate, flawed, and utterly fascinating. She made mistakes, yes, but she lived."

Emma snorted. "She also died quite dramatically, if I recall correctly."

"Details, details," Stella waved her hand dismissively. "The point is, she wasn't afraid to take risks, to follow her heart—even if it led to ruin. There's something admirable about that."

"Or completely reckless," Emma muttered, though a part of her was intrigued. Maybe there was more to this trip than she had initially thought. If all of what Stella was telling her was true, it meant the worst was already behind her. Emma looked forward to the strength and wisdom she could glean from this escapade. Looking out of the small square window, Yonville did not appear to be a popular tourist destination to say the least.

As the train pulled into Yonville, Stella stood and adjusted her beret, looking every bit the regal matron. "Come, Emma. Let's see what mischief we can uncover."

The train rattled to a halt at Yonville, and Emma stepped out onto the platform, taking in the sights. The town had an air of quiet charm, its cobblestone streets winding through quaint, old buildings that seemed to whisper secrets of the past. The war had left its mark on Yonville, but the town had been lovingly restored over the years. The buildings were now fresh with pastel facades, and the town square boasted a quiet market bustling with locals and tourists alike.

Stella and Emma strolled through the streets, the crisp morning air filled with the scent of freshly baked bread and blooming flowers. "Let's get those croissants" Stella said with complete unwavering focus. Emma laughed to herself. They made their way to the town's small museum, a humble yet dignified building standing proudly amidst the more modern structures.

As they entered the museum, the curator greeted them warmly and led them to the section that was dedicated to the residents of the 1850s. It was before the World Wars and it discussed the building of the town, including the acquisition of a country doctor, Charles Bovary. The walls were lined with portraits, letters, and artifacts from the 19th century, each piece telling a fragment of Emma Bovary's bored existence.

Stella's eyes lit up as she spotted a large, framed photograph hanging prominently on the wall. "Ah, there she is," she murmured, guiding Emma closer.

The photograph was of their ancestor, Emma Bovary, a strikingly beautiful woman with an aristocratic air. She was dressed in elegant, expensive clothing, her posture graceful and refined. Yet, despite her outward appearance of wealth and sophistication, her eyes betrayed a deep sense of ennui. She looked disengaged, almost bored, as if the trappings of her affluent life held no meaning for her.

Emma stared at the photograph, captivated by the woman who shared her name. "She looks so...unfulfilled," she remarked quietly. "Was she afraid?"

Stella nodded, a hint of sadness in her voice. "Yes, she was always searching for something more, something to fill the void within her, yet never really going for it." Emma continued to study the photograph, feeling a strange connection to the woman in the picture. "Do you think she ever found what she was looking for?"

Stella sighed, her eyes fixed on her daughter. "Perhaps, in fleeting moments. But ultimately, she was a prisoner of her own desires. Her story is a cautionary tale, but also a reminder of the human need for fulfillment and meaning."

Stella sighed, a mixture of frustration and concern swirling within her as she watched her granddaughter, Emma, navigate the museum. They had come here hoping for a meaningful connection, a bridge between generations, but Emma seemed distant, absorbed in analyzing each exhibit rather than experiencing them with an open heart.

"Emma, darling, isn't this painting exquisite?" Stella asked, gesturing toward a vibrant canvas depicting a bustling marketplace. She had hoped it would stir something within Emma, evoke a shared moment of awe or appreciation.

Emma nodded thoughtfully, her brow furrowed in contemplation. "It's fascinating, Grandma. The artist's use of color and perspective is quite impressive."

Stella's heart sank slightly. She had yearned for Emma to feel the same emotional resonance she did—to see not just the technique, but the soul behind the art. They continued through the museum, each step echoing with Stella's silent prayers for a breakthrough, a spark of connection.

As they reached a sculpture garden bathed in dappled sunlight, Stella paused beside a marble figure of a mother and child. She touched its smooth surface gently, feeling the coolness beneath her fingertips. "Emma, look at the tenderness in this sculpture. Can you feel the love the artist poured into it?"

Emma studied the sculpture intently, her expression thoughtful. "I can appreciate the craftsmanship, Grandma. The detail is incredible."

Stella sighed inwardly, realizing how much Emma's analytical mind was keeping her from truly experiencing the art's emotional depth. She glanced around the serene garden, the sculptures standing like silent witnesses to her silent plea.

"Dear God," Stella whispered silently, her voice carrying her earnest prayer into the air. "Grant Emma the gift of seeing with her heart, not just her mind. Help her to feel the beauty and passion that surrounds us."

They moved on to other exhibits, but the image of Emma Bovary lingered in Emma's mind. She saw reflections of herself in her ancestor's restless spirit and wondered if she, too, was destined to search endlessly for something that might never be found. Stella acted as if she were about to punch herself playfully before Emma turned to look at her inquisitively.

After a thorough exploration of the museum, Stella suggested they take a break at a nearby café. They settled at a small table by the window, sipping coffee and watching the world go by. The café was quaint, with a cozy atmosphere that invited conversation and contemplation.

Stella leaned in, her voice soft. "You know, Emma, there's a reason I wanted to bring you here. I see so much of her in you—the same drive, the same longing for something more. But I also see a chance for you to learn from her mistakes, to find a balance between ambition and contentment."

Emma nodded slowly, absorbing her grandmother's words. "I hope so. Sometimes I feel like I'm constantly chasing something, but I'm not even sure what it is."

Stella reached across the table and squeezed Emma's hand. "You're young, and you have your whole life ahead of you. Just remember to appreciate what you have while striving for what you want. And never forget, you come from a long line of strong, passionate women."

As they finished their coffee and prepared to explore more of Yonville, Emma felt a renewed sense of purpose. The visit to the museum had given her a deeper understanding of her heritage and a clearer perspective on her own life. She was determined to honor her ancestor's legacy while forging her own path, one that balanced ambition with appreciation for the present.

The day stretched ahead of them, filled with promise and possibility. Emma and Stella stepped back out into the sunlight, ready to embrace whatever adventures awaited them in this charming, historical town.

As they continued their exploration of Yonville, the quaint streets and picturesque scenery providing a perfect backdrop for their conversation, Stella began to share more about the story of their infamous ancestor, Emma Bovary.

"Charles, Emma's husband, hoped that moving to the village of Yonville-l'Abbaye would lift her spirits," Stella began, her voice taking on a nostalgic tone. "He was a kind and devoted man, but he never truly understood the depth of Emma's restlessness. She was much younger and more ignorant than his previous wife. He found it refreshing and was blind to her passions."

Emma listened intently, picturing the scenes her grandmother described. The village had a timeless quality to it, as if the echoes of the past still lingered there.

"Charles believed that a change of scenery might be just what she needed," Stella continued. "But Emma's dissatisfaction ran deeper than mere geography. The move to Yonville did little to alleviate her growing unhappiness."

They wandered into a small park, where children played and couples strolled hand in hand. The vibrant life around them contrasted starkly with the story of Emma Bovary's inner turmoil.

"In Yonville, Emma met new people, including Léon, a young law clerk with whom she developed a close friendship," Stella said, her eyes scanning the park as if searching for remnants of the past. "Their connection sparked something in her—a sense of excitement and possibility that she had been missing."

Emma looked down. *This must be where it went downhill for her,* she thought.

Emma Bovary's story unfolded like a tragic novel, each chapter filled with longing and disillusionment. "But even Léon couldn't fill the void within her," Stella added. "She turned to other means of escape, accumulating debts and pursuing affairs in a desperate attempt to find fulfillment."

Oh no, Emma secretly lamented. She was also financially illiterate! Trying to maintain the balance of having her own thoughts and also trying to avoid being critical of her own ancestor, she moved on. As they continued to walk, Stella's voice softened. "The irony is that Emma had everything most people would dream of—beauty, a loving husband, and a comfortable life. But she couldn't see it. She was always searching for something just out of reach, something she couldn't quite grasp."

Emma thought about her own life, her own desires and ambitions. The parallels between her and her ancestor were striking. She wondered if she, too, was chasing an elusive dream. They paused by a small fountain, the water sparkling in the sunlight. "Emma's story is a reminder that contentment comes from within," Stella said, placing a gentle hand on Emma's shoulder. "No matter where you go or what you have, it's your perspective that shapes your happiness."

Emma nodded, feeling a deep connection to the woman she was named after. "Thank you for sharing this with me, Grandma," she said sincerely. "It gives me a lot to think about."

Stella smiled warmly. "I'm glad. Now, let's continue our adventure. Yonville has much more to offer, and I want to show you everything."

The village of Yonville-l'Abbaye, with its rich history and timeless charm, had left an indelible mark on Emma. It was a place where she could reflect on her own journey and find the inspiration to forge her own path, one that honored her heritage while embracing the possibilities of the future.

After the square, they made their way to the Normandy Beach, a place of both natural beauty and historical significance. The beach was serene, the waves gently lapping at the shore as if whispering secrets of the past. Emma and Stella walked along the sand, their conversation turning to the harrowing events of World War II.

"This beach, you know," Stella began, her voice tinged with reverence, "was one of the sites of the D-Day landings. Right before I was born, this area was a battlefield, part of the famous Battle of Normandy."

Emma looked out at the expanse of ocean, trying to imagine the chaos and courage that had unfolded here. "It's hard to believe such tranquility hides such a turbulent history."

Stella nodded, her eyes distant. "Many lives were lost, but it marked a turning point in the war. The bravery of those soldiers... it's something we should never forget."

They continued their walk, stopping at a small, solemn memorial dedicated to the soldiers who fought and died during the battle. The names etched in stone served as a stark reminder of the cost of freedom. One name stood out to Emma, Pedro Kettering. *Huh,* she thought. *Same last name as Franz.*

As they sat in deep contemplation, Emma turned to Stella. "Do you think we can ever escape the past, or are we always bound to it in some way?"

Stella sighed, a hint of sadness in her eyes. "I think the past shapes us, but it doesn't have to define us. We can learn from it, grow from it, and hopefully, make different choices. You both married doctors, now that is something, you know?" Stella asked.

"Antoinie and I used to come to this very beach. His family helped fund the French military that fought for freedom from the Nazis with their banking legacy. He was a hero in his own way." Stella sighed to herself. Antonie had grown up in Paris, and loved coming to the beach to remind himself of his powerful past. From the beach, they would go to the hotel in Yonville and spend countless days curled up in each other's arms. Stella loved the freedom from America's conservative value system and loved Antonie's attention and charms. She also loved knowing she was spending time in the town that her grandmother Berthe was born in.

Emma could see the look of love and strength in Stella's far-off gaze. She didn't know her grandfather well, but she grew to love him through Stella's stories. With a resigned sigh, Emma helped Stella back onto the train where they napped until they reached the depot in Paris.

As Emma and Stella strolled back to their hotel, they walked in comfortable silence, each absorbed in their thoughts. Once they were settled in the cozy sitting room of their suite, Emma turned to Stella with a curious expression.

"Tell me more about Charles," Emma said, her voice soft yet insistent. "I feel like I need to understand him better to understand myself."

Stella smiled gently, nodding as she leaned back in her chair. "Charles was your great-great-great-grandfather. He was the country doctor, much like Franz in his dedication and earnestness, but their similarities end there."

Emma leaned forward, her interest piqued. "How so?"

"Charles was a simple man, perhaps too simple for Emma," Stella began, her eyes distant as she conjured memories of stories passed down through the generations. "He adored her, doted on her even, but he was oblivious to her deeper needs and desires. He believed that providing for her material comfort was enough, never realizing that she craved something more—adventure, passion, excitement."

Emma frowned slightly, thinking of Franz. "Franz is attentive and loving, but in a way that feels more balanced. He encourages my ambitions and shares my dreams. Was Charles not supportive?"

"He was, in his own way," Stella replied, choosing her words carefully. "But his support was often misplaced. He thought that moving to a new town or buying her a new dress would solve her discontent. He never truly understood that her dissatisfaction was deeper, rooted in her longing for unfulfilled dreams and ambitions. During that time, women were not encouraged enough to reach for the sky and embrace their dreams. There simply was a lack of role models and diversity.

Emma nodded slowly, contemplating the contrast. Stella smiled, a hint of pride in her eyes. "And that is why your relationship with Franz is so different. Charles loved Emma, but he loved her in the only way he knew how. Franz loves you in a way that acknowledges and respects who you are as a person. You were already self-actualized before you met him."

They sat in silence for a moment, the weight of their conversation settling over them. Emma thought of Franz, appreciating the depth of their connection and the mutual respect they shared.

"Charles was a good man," Stella continued softly, "but he was not the right man for Emma. He provided stability and security, but he could never give her the passion and excitement she craved."

Emma looked at Stella, her eyes shining with gratitude. "Thank you for sharing this with me. It helps me appreciate what I have with Franz even more."

Stella reached out and took Emma's hand, squeezing it gently. "I'm glad, my dear. Understanding our past helps us shape our future. And I have no doubt that you and Franz will build a wonderful future together." Emma did not fully realize the impact of what Stella was saying at this moment.

As they sat together, their bond strengthened by their shared history and newfound understanding, Emma felt a sense of peace. She knew that, unlike her ancestor, she had the opportunity to create a life filled with love, passion, and fulfillment. And it was her responsibility not to lose it.

Stella sat across from Emma in their cozy Parisian suite, the soft glow of the lamp casting a warm ambiance over the room. The day had been filled with revelations and reflections, and now, as they settled in, Stella felt it was time to delve deeper into the story of Charles and Emma.

"Charles comes from a long line of aristocrats," Stella began, her voice steady and thoughtful. "His mother, Madame Bovary Senior, was a formidable woman. Strong-willed and traditional, she believed in upholding societal norms and expectations without question. Especially since her own life had been torn to shreds by her louse of a husband."

Emma listened intently, her eyes focused on Stella. She knew of Charles's background vaguely but had never fully understood its implications. She could tell that her grandmother Emma must have been an admirer of Madame Bovary Senior.

"Madame Bovary Senior had high hopes for Charles," Stella continued, her expression tinged with empathy. "She expected him to marry a suitable woman from a respectable family, someone who would uphold their social standing and support him in his career as a doctor."

Emma nodded slowly, sensing the weight of societal expectations pressing down on Charles and Emma.

"Charles deeply loved Emma," Stella emphasized, her voice softening with compassion. "He saw her beauty, her intelligence, and her spirit, and he believed that bringing her to Yonville would make her happy."

Emma furrowed her brow, recalling her own dreams and aspirations that sometimes clashed with Franz's upbringing and expectations.

"Charles's inability to understand Emma's desires," Stella continued, "coupled with his devotion to his mother's expectations, created a rift in their marriage. Emma longed for passion, romance, and a life beyond the confines of provincial Yonville. She felt stifled by the demands life placed on her, and she didn't have a way to cope with it."

The room fell into a thoughtful silence as Emma absorbed Stella's words. She could empathize with Emma Bovary's plight, feeling the weight of societal constraints that had shaped her ancestor's life.

Stella sat, swirling a glass of Bordeaux with a thoughtful expression. Emma, her granddaughter, had always been a puzzle to her—a blend of independence and vulnerability that seemed to mirror her own turbulent past.

"You know, Emma," Stella began, her voice tinged with a hint of dark humor, "your ancestor Emma was raised by nuns after her own mother's passing. Strong women, those nuns. But they're not exactly maternal."

Emma, wanting to be a mother herself, was grateful for Grandma Stella's guidance. She and Stella both looked at each other with a hopeful smile. "Grandpa Antonie was your escape, wasn't he?" Emma coaxed, looking at Stella's glass.

Stella chuckled wryly, memories of her affair with Emma's grandfather surfacing like old photographs. "Antonie was a devilishly charming man," she admitted, swirling her wine thoughtfully. "We'd sneak off to cafes, pretending we were in some grand love story straight out of Balzac. Yonville was our haven, a brief respite from reality."

"But you see, my dear," Stella continued, her tone turning more serious, "You will be the best mother you can be because you have to be. Do not let that sense of duty rain on your parade."

Emma nodded slowly, absorbing Stella's words.

Stella shrugged elegantly, taking a sip of her wine. "Who knows, my dear? Life's a comedy, isn't it? Here I am, the grande dame of Paris, dispensing wisdom over a glass of Bordeaux. And there you are, my clever granddaughter, navigating the world with a nun's discipline and your own stubbornness."

As they sat in comfortable silence, the weight of their shared history hung in the air like the scent of roses in bloom. Stella knew that while their paths had diverged, they were forever bound by the threads of family and fate—two strong-willed women alone in the world together.

Over breakfast the next morning, with sunlight streaming through the windows and the aroma of freshly brewed coffee filling the air, Emma listened intently as Stella, her 104-year-old grandmother, began to recount a tale from her youth.

Stella, her silver hair neatly pulled back, paused thoughtfully as she stirred her tea. "You know, back in the 1970s, I was in Paris with Anotonie," she began, her voice carrying the weight of years gone by. "We stumbled upon this fascinating clock."

"It had diamonds instead of numbers and it was encrusted in gold."

"Now that's bougie," Emma added with a twinkle in her eye, a phrase she often used to describe anything ostentatiously luxurious or pretentious.

As Emma listened to Stella's tale, she couldn't help but marvel at the wisdom and perspective gained over a century of living. Stella's story of Emma resonated deeply, reminding her of the complexities of human desires and the importance of authenticity in navigating life's choices. Emma cherished not only the story of Emma but also the bond she shared with her wise grandmother, whose tales of love, betrayal, and life's lessons would continue to inspire her for years to come.

As they sat together, enveloped in the quietude of their thoughts, Emma felt a renewed appreciation for her husband, Franz, and the understanding they shared. She knew that, unlike Emma Bovary, she had the freedom and support to pursue her dreams while navigating the complexities of their heritage. And for that, she was deeply grateful.

Emma had always been one to revisit old wounds, hoping that somehow, understanding the past better might change the present. But this time, in the enchanting city of Paris, she decided it was different. The weight of previous heartbreaks and betrayals felt less significant here, among the bustling streets and romantic ambiance. Emma made a conscious choice to let sleeping dogs lie, to not dig up the old sorrows that had long settled. She resolved to embrace the beauty of the present and let the past be the past, untouched and undisturbed.

Stella watched Emma closely. She could see the gears turning in her daughter's mind, processing all the new experiences and emotions Paris was evoking. The city had a way of making one introspective, and Emma was no exception. The Eiffel Tower, the Seine, the quaint cafes—they all seemed to be weaving a spell around her, making her more open and yet more guarded at the same time.

Stella had her own secrets to bear. She had learned about Antonie's past, a history tangled with complexities and shadows that Emma was unaware of. Stella knew that revealing Antonie's past now might disrupt the delicate balance Emma was finding in Paris. She decided it was best to wait, to give Emma a few more days to soak in the magic of the city without the burden of this new information.

Leon adjusted his tie and took a deep breath as he stood outside Emma's hotel. The city lights reflected in the glass doors, casting a warm glow on his chiseled features. He smoothed his hair and stepped inside, feeling a mix of excitement and anticipation. Tonight was going to be unforgettable.

The lobby of the five-star hotel exuded elegance, with its marble floors and opulent chandeliers. Leon's eyes scanned the area until they landed on Emma, who was descending the grand staircase. She looked stunning in a black cocktail dress that hugged her curves perfectly, her soft hair cascading in loose waves over her shoulders.

"Emma," Leon called, his voice filled with admiration. "You look absolutely breathtaking."

Emma smiled, her eyes sparkling with a mix of confidence and mischief. "Thank you, Leon. You clean up pretty well yourself."

He extended his arm, and she took it, their connection immediate and electric. Together, they stepped out into the night, the cool breeze adding a touch of exhilaration to their evening.

Leon had planned every detail meticulously. They arrived at a chic rooftop bar, where the city sprawled out below them like a sea of lights. The atmosphere was vibrant, the music pulsating with energy, but had nothing on Emma's allure. Leon ordered them both cocktails, and they settled into a cozy corner with a view of the skyline.

The dim light of the rooftop bar cast long shadows across the marble floor, creating an eerie ambiance. Leon and Emma sat at a secluded table, the flickering candlelight reflecting in their drinks. The city below them hummed with life, oblivious to the strange dance of emotions unfolding above.

Leon swirled his drink, watching the liquid catch the light like liquid obsidian. "You know, Emma, there's something about you that feels... timeless," he said, his voice low and tinged with curiosity.

Emma raised an eyebrow, a playful smirk curling her lips. "Timeless, you say? Do you think I might be some ancient slug?"

Leon chuckled, but there was a dark edge to his laughter. "Who knows? Maybe you are. Maybe I'm about to become your next victim."

Emma leaned closer, her eyes glinting with a mischievous light. "And if I were? What then, Leon? Would you run away in fear?"

He met her gaze, his heart pounding in his chest. "No," he said, his voice barely more than a whisper. "I think I'd stay. I think I'd want to know more."

"Do you believe in ghosts, Leon?" Emma asked, her voice soft and melodic, like a siren's call.

Leon took a sip of his drink, considering her question. "I believe in the ghosts we carry with us," he replied. "The memories and regrets that haunt our minds. The shadows that linger in our hearts. Perhaps we can outrun them?" He toyed with her.

Emma nodded, her expression thoughtful. "That's a beautifully tragic way to see it," she said. "But what if I told you that some ghosts are real? That they walk among us, unseen but always present?"

Leon felt a shiver run down his spine. "Are you trying to scare me, Emma?"

The chemistry between them was undeniable, a magnetic pull that drew them closer despite the darkness that seemed to surround them. Leon's desire for Emma grew with each passing moment, an almost primal urge that he could barely control.

As the night deepened, they moved to a quieter corner of the bar, the shadows wrapping around them like a velvet shroud. Leon's hand found its way to Emma's, their fingers intertwining in a silent promise.

"You fascinate me, Emma," he confessed, his voice raw with longing. "I can't explain it, but I feel like I've known you forever."

Emma's eyes softened, and for a moment, Leon thought he saw a flicker of vulnerability in her gaze. "Forever is a long time, Leon," she murmured.

Before he could respond, she leaned in, her lips brushing against his ear. "Tell me, Leon," she whispered, her breath hot against his skin. "What would you do to have me?"

Leon's pulse quickened, his desire for her burning hotter than ever. "Anything," he breathed. "I'd do anything."

Emma pulled back slightly, her eyes locking onto his. "Even if it meant walking through the gates of hell?"

There was a moment of tense silence, the weight of her words hanging heavy in the air. Leon's mind raced, torn between reason and the intoxicating allure of this mysterious woman. Finally, he made his decision.

"Even then," he said firmly.

They left the bar together, the cool night air wrapping around them like a lover's embrace. As they walked through the deserted streets, the city seemed to transform, its familiar landmarks taking on an eerie, otherworldly quality. They moved on to an exclusive nightclub, where the bass thumped in time with their racing hearts. The dance floor was a kaleidoscope of colors and bodies, and Leon led Emma through the crowd, his hand resting possessively on her lower back.

They danced together, the music enveloping them in its seductive rhythm. Leon's hands roamed over Emma's body, his touch both bold and respectful. He leaned in, his lips brushing against her ear. "I can't take my eyes off you," he whispered, his voice husky with desire.

Emma met his gaze, her expression a mix of amusement and temptation. "Leon, you're quite the charmer," she replied, her voice playful.

As the night wore on, Leon's desire for Emma only intensified. He pulled her closer, his hands tracing the curve of her waist. "Emma, I want you," he confessed, his voice raw with longing.

"Let's get out of here."

Emma's eyes sparkled with a mix of mischief and determination. She placed a hand on his chest, gently pushing him back. "Leon, you're sweet, but tonight isn't about that," she said firmly.

Leon blinked, caught off guard by her rejection. "But I thought—"

She cut him off with a knowing smile. "I know what you thought. But let's keep things professional, shall we?"

Leon felt a wave of frustration and embarrassment wash over him. He took a step back, running a hand through his hair. "Emma, I'm sorry if I misread things."

Emma's expression softened. "It's okay, Leon. You're a great guy, and I had a wonderful time tonight." With that, they awkwardly decided to call it a night. Emma still had one trick up her sleeve, and she was determined to use it. She felt like the most powerful woman on earth.

When they reached Emma's hotel, she turned to him, her expression unreadable. "This is where we part ways," she said, her voice tinged with a sadness that felt ancient and profound.

Leon felt a pang of disappointment. "Will I see you again?"

Emma's smile was wistful. "Perhaps. But remember, Leon, some doors, once opened, can never be closed."

With that, she slipped inside, leaving Leon standing alone in the darkness, his mind swirling with a mix of desire, fear, and curiosity. He knew that tonight had changed him, had opened his eyes to a world he had never imagined.

"Leon, there's something you should know," she said, her tone cautious. "I found out that you're the Marketing Director at Peach, Inc."

Leon stared at her, stunned. "How did you—"

She raised a hand, stopping him. "Let's just say, I have my ways. This makes things a bit... complicated, don't you think?"

Leon nodded slowly, the reality of their situation sinking in. "Yeah, I guess it does."

Emma gave him a small smile. "Goodnight, Leon. And thank you for a memorable evening."

With that, she slipped inside her room, leaving Leon standing in the entryway, his mind swirling with conflicting emotions. As he walked away, he couldn't shake the feeling that this was far from the end of their story.

Emma went in with a sigh. She could not believe she survived an evening with her biggest competitor.

"I thought you would never get home." Stella said, sitting in the dark. Her recliner was filled with large plush blankets, a cucumber eye mask, a knitting basket, and a vodka tonic. She looked like she was joking when she quickly stood up and used her knitting light to peer into Emma's bloodshot eyes.

"Holy Molasses, we have to get you fixed up for tomorrow's expo quick!"

Emma laughed. She pliantly sat down in front of the bathroom mirror, allowing Stella to draw her a bath. As Emma changed out of her dress and sat her shoes aside, Stella began to ask her some serious questions.

"How did our handsome man take the news that not only are you married, but that we know about his dirty little secret." Stella was referring to the fact that he worked for Peach, Inc.

"Well, let's just say I kept my vows intact." Emma began. Stella looked at her with a silent appreciation, and then went back to filling her tub with Epsom salt and lavender.

"I have not known someone as creative and forward thinking as he, though." Emma again mused to herself.

"That is great, dear. Tomorrow, why will he not be giving any speeches?" Stella asked.

Emma thought about this for a moment. "Well, I suppose that he is not as highly revered or accomplished as I originally thought. Maybe there is some wiggle room to get in with his higher-ups and see just what my competition is up to." Emma was lost in thought as she dipped her toes into her luxe bath and sat down in the bubbles, ever so gracefully.

Stella sat back in her Kitten Kiss pajamas, and let out a bellowing sigh. "That's the spirit!" She gave Emma a grin and then shut the door behind her. She knew Emma would be in there for a while. Sitting back down with her knitting needles, Stella pondered her life. Her own mother had shielded her from the truths about her past until she was around Emma's age, too. Stella loved to think about the knowledge and power that her great-grandmother possessed. She clearly didn't fit in with the bourgeois of the time, and she must not have felt very welcome by Madame Bovary Senior. Perhaps Emma's greatest contribution to society was Berthe. Perhaps Emma ended it all in a fit of despair, but deep down thought it was her greatest act of love.

Stella knew better thanks to her mother. Life was not our art to play with, judge, or criticize. It did not belong to us. On her worst days, Stella thought about how her ancestors would cringe at the absurdities of the modern world. On her best days, she looked forward to even her most mundane tasks. She said a silent prayer hoping that this wisdom would reach through the bathroom door and flood Emma's senses.

Part 3

In Paris, where the Seine flows with timeless grace, A wealthy banker's tale comes to its final place. His legacy, a secret, hidden from the light, unfolds in quiet whispers, revealing in the night. He dreamed of meeting her, his daughter unknown, yet fate dealt its hand, and now he's overthrown. His wealth, a silent witness to his hidden past, now entrusted to Stella, the keeper steadfast.

Stella, lone survivor in the banker's kin, grasps the weight of fortune, where to begin? Emma, unaware, finds Paris' charm divine, her days unfurling in its cafes and wine. But fate twists again with news so unforeseen, a life begins anew, in the midst of the scene. Emma, pregnant, with dreams now rearranged, faces the future, emotions deeply estranged.

The Parisian air, once a haven so grand, now echoes with questions, futures unplanned. As Stella passes down what the banker bestowed, Emma's journey of discovery takes its bold road. In this tale of wealth, secrets, and surprise, Paris witnesses truths under its azure skies. Emma's path, now intertwined with legacy's embrace, navigates the twists of fate, with courage and grace.

Lost in a world of imagination, Emma sat upright in the tub. A pervasive idea came together for her. Her mother died for her.

"Of course she did!" Emma exclaimed to herself, feeling a bit timid.

Her aristocratic heritage was marred with sin, affluence, hope. And what for? She knew deep down that it was for the betterment of humanity, hers in particular. She had come from millions of people and

Jesus Christ himself, no doubt. In this moment, Emma knew she could conquer any mountain in her path.

"Oh I am not a lazy housewife, no. I am going to break the world with my next move!" She smiled to herself, letting the bathwater trickle over her face. Standing up and demonstrating a strength not known to mankind, she clothed herself and walked back into the bedroom where Stella sat.

"What are you thinking about, dear?" Stella asks politely.

"My future." Marrying Franz brought out this side of her. Emma picked up the romance she was reading, Love of My After Life. *Emma liked to read*, Emma thought in the corner of her mind. Pushing the thought away she continued silently until the wee hours of the morning. As she read and soon fell asleep, Stella watched her adult daughter with love and care. She was blessed to be a centenarian who was adored by her children. Soon, she too, fell asleep.

The grand hall of the Palais des Congrès in Paris buzzed with anticipation the next morning. The annual Parisian Marketing Expo was in full swing, a vibrant gathering of industry leaders, innovators, and enthusiasts from around the world. The air was filled with the hum of excited conversations, the clinking of glasses, and the occasional burst of laughter.

As attendees milled about, the hall itself stood as a testament to the importance of the event. Towering ceilings arched high above, adorned with intricate moldings and chandeliers that cast a warm, inviting glow over the sea of booths and displays. Banners and signs in vibrant colors announced the presence of major corporations and startups alike, each vying for attention in the bustling marketplace of ideas.

Emma navigated through the throng, her eyes wide with curiosity and excitement. She had always found these expos exhilarating, a place where creativity and business acumen collided in the most fascinating ways. Dressed in a tailored suit that spoke of both professionalism and style, she felt confident and ready to absorb every bit of knowledge and inspiration the event had to offer.

She paused at a booth featuring an interactive digital display. The company was showcasing their latest AI-driven marketing analytics tool, a sleek piece of technology that promised to revolutionize the way businesses understood and engaged with their audiences. Emma engaged in a lively discussion with the representative, asking pointed questions and sharing her own insights. It was a dynamic exchange, one that left her feeling both challenged and inspired.

Moving on, Emma spotted a familiar face in the crowd. It was Leon. He greeted her with a warm smile and a glass of champagne, which she accepted gratefully.

"Emma! It's been too long," Leon exclaimed teasingly, raising his glass in a toast.

"Indeed, it has," Emma replied, clinking her glass against his. Her sleek silhouette captured his attention. "How have you been?"

"Busy as ever," Leon said with a chuckle. "But isn't that the nature of our work? Always something new to chase, always another innovation on the horizon."

They chatted for a while, catching up on personal and professional news. Their conversation was a perfect blend of camaraderie and professional respect, a reminder of the tight-knit community that the marketing world could be.

As they spoke, a hush fell over the hall. The lights dimmed slightly, and a spotlight focused on the main stage. The keynote speaker was about to begin. Emma, the keynote speaker was a renowned futurist and marketing guru, known for his ability to predict trends and inspire innovation. She took the stage with a commanding presence, her voice resonating through the hall as she spoke about the future of marketing in an increasingly digital and connected world.

"L'analyse statistique," she began, her voice clear and engaging, "n'est pas seulement un outil. C'est une boussole, une carte, et un guide pour naviguer dans le vaste océan des données. Aujourd'hui, je vais vous montrer comment créer une toile de stratégie qui vous permettra de prédire, d'influencer et de conquérir."

As Emma delved into her presentation, the audience hung on her every word. She spoke of the power of predictive analytics, the importance of understanding customer behavior, and the ways in which data could be woven into a cohesive, actionable strategy. Her insights were sharp, her examples relevant, and her delivery impeccable.

"...Et enfin, n'oubliez jamais que derrière chaque donnée, il y a une histoire humaine. C'est cette histoire qui donne vie à nos stratégies et nous permet de toucher véritablement nos clients."

As she concluded her speech, the audience erupted into applause. Emma smiled, a sense of accomplishment washing over her. She had captivated them, and now, it was time to mingle and make connections.

Leon was among the first to approach her, his eyes shining with admiration. "Emma, c'était incroyable," he said, his voice filled with genuine enthusiasm. "Vous avez vraiment capté l'attention de tout le monde."

Emma laughed softly. "Merci, Leon. Ça me fait plaisir de l'entendre."

Leon took a step closer, lowering his voice slightly. "Je voulais vous féliciter en personne. Et, si cela vous intéresse, j'aimerais vous présenter mon patron chez Peach, Inc."

Emma raised an eyebrow, intrigued. "Ça serait un plaisir. Allons-y."

Leon led her through the bustling expo, past booths adorned with cutting-edge technology and interactive displays. They moved through a crowd of elegantly dressed professionals, their conversations a symphony of French, English, and a myriad of other languages.

As they approached the Peach, Inc. booth, the atmosphere shifted. The booth was a sleek, modern affair, with clean lines and a minimalist design. Large screens showcased the latest in marketing technology, and a group of well-dressed executives mingled with potential clients.

Leon introduced Emma to his boss, a distinguished man with silver hair and a sharp suit. "Emma, je vous présente Monsieur Dupont, notre directeur général."

Monsieur Dupont extended his hand, his smile genuine. "Enchanté, Emma. Leon m'a beaucoup parlé de vous."

Emma shook his hand, her grip firm. "Le plaisir est pour moi, Monsieur Dupont. J'ai entendu parler de vos innovations chez Peach, Inc., et je suis impatiente d'en savoir plus."

Their conversation flowed easily, touching on the latest trends in marketing and the future of data analytics. Emma's insights impressed Monsieur Dupont, and she found herself feeling a sense of camaraderie with these new acquaintances.

Suddenly, the lights dimmed, and a spotlight illuminated the stage at the far end of the hall. The crowd began to murmur with excitement as the unmistakable beat of Megan Thee Stallion's hit song "Savage" filled the air. The rapper herself appeared on stage, her presence commanding and electrifying.

"Megan Thee Stallion à l'Expo Marketing, ça, c'est une surprise," Leon said with a grin.

Emma's eyes sparkled with amusement. "Ils savent vraiment comment faire un show."

As Megan Thee Stallion took the stage, the energy in the room surged like a caffeine overdose at a marketing exec's third meeting of the day. The crowd, a mix of besuited professionals and artful hipsters, erupted into a cacophony of cheers and half-hearted attempts at dancing. Her powerful lyrics boomed through the speakers, reverberating off the sterile walls of the convention center, each word a testament to the unholy fusion of art and marketing.

It was a peculiar sight: the audience, who usually calculated engagement metrics and return on investment, were now caught in the throes of Megan's dynamic performance. The lights flashed in sync with the beat, casting the room in shades of red and blue, reminiscent of a crime scene investigation. For a moment, the sterile, data-driven world of marketing was drenched in the vibrant chaos of raw creativity.

One particularly enthusiastic marketing director, with the energy of a hamster on a wheel, attempted to twerk, much to the amusement (and horror) of his colleagues. It was a reminder that in this industry, creativity was just as crucial as data—though perhaps not everyone should attempt to express it through dance.

Amidst the spectacle, Leon watched with a bemused smile. He'd spent countless hours crunching numbers and analyzing trends, but seeing Megan command the stage was a potent reminder of the visceral power of creativity. It was the kind of performance that could turn the most mundane product launch into a viral sensation or make a boring brand seem suddenly desirable.

As the performance continued, Leon's mind wandered to the endless spreadsheets waiting for him back at the office. He wondered if he could convince his boss that incorporating twerking into their next ad campaign might boost engagement. Probably not, but it was a tempting thought.

The juxtaposition of the sterile, calculated world of marketing with Megan's unapologetically bold performance was almost poetic. Here was an artist who embodied the very essence of creativity, reminding everyone in the room that no matter how much they relied on data and statistics, it was the unpredictable, the raw, and the unfiltered that truly captivated audiences.

When Megan finally finished her set, the applause was thunderous. As the lights dimmed and the room returned to its previous state of corporate decorum, Leon couldn't help but chuckle. Marketing, he realized, was a strange beast—an industry that thrived on the delicate balance between the predictable world of data and the wild, untamed realm of creativity.

The performance ended with a standing ovation, and the crowd slowly began to disperse, returning to the business of the expo. Emma turned to Leon, a smile playing on her lips.

"Merci pour cette soirée, Leon. C'était vraiment exceptionnel."

Leon returned her smile, his eyes filled with admiration. "C'était un plaisir, Emma. J'espère que nous aurons l'occasion de collaborer à l'avenir."

As they parted ways, Emma felt a sense of exhilaration. The expo had been a resounding success, and she had made valuable connections that could shape the future of her career. The night air was cool as she stepped out of the Palais des Congrès, the lights of Paris twinkling around her.

Walking back to her hotel, Emma couldn't help but feel a sense of anticipation for what lay ahead. The world of marketing was vast and ever-changing, but with the right strategies and a touch of creativity, anything was possible. And tonight, she had taken another step towards mastering that world.

The streets of Paris were alive with the bustling energy of a summer afternoon, but to Emma, the world felt as cold and desolate as a forgotten graveyard. She stepped off the tram, her heels clicking against the cement, her mind a whirl of doubt and regret. The grand façade of their hotel building loomed ahead, an imposing reminder of the life she was about to leave behind once her trip ended.

Franz had made it clear he wasn't happy with the way she was spending her time in Paris. Her escapades, her attempts to reclaim a sense of freedom and identity, had only driven a wedge between them. She had tried to explain, to make him see that she needed more than the role of a housewife, but the words had fallen flat. Now, as she climbed the steps to her room, the weight of his disappointment settled over her like a shroud.

The view of the city was beautiful, but it did little to lift her spirits. She thought about the life she had envisioned, the dreams she had chased, and the reality she now faced. The financial strain of her endeavors weighed heavily on her mind. The fear of going broke, of losing everything, was a constant, gnawing presence. Marrying Franz did little to lift her financial worries.

But it was the guilt that hurt the most. The guilt of almost cheating on Franz, of possibly betraying the man who was fatefully loyal to her. She had tried to justify it, to tell herself that she needed an escape, that she deserved some happiness. But the guilt lingered, festering like an open wound.

Emma closed her eyes and took a deep breath. Whatever happened, she wanted Franz to be proud of her. She wanted to make things right, to find a way back to him that would pleasantly surprise him. If she couldn't think herself out of the paper bag that was her life, what good was she at marketing or anything else? Sensing that she was becoming too hard on herself, she took a deep breath, just like her grandmother taught her to do.

The sound of her phone chirping caught her off guard. It was her husband.

"Hi," he said, his voice soft.

"Hi," she replied, forcing a smile in return.

There was a moment of awkward silence, the air thick with unspoken words.

"How was your day?" he asked, his tone neutral.

"It was fine," Emma said, though it was a lie. "I had my keynote speech today."

"Good," Franz said absently, staring out the window of their lonely Brooklyn brownstone.

Emma bit her lip, the words she wanted to say stuck in her throat. She wanted to tell him how much she loved him, how sorry she was for everything. But the fear of his reaction held her back.

"Franz," she began hesitantly. "I... I want to make things right. I want you to be proud of me."

He turned to the phone, his expression unreadable. "Emma, it's not about being proud. It's about trust. It's about us."

She nodded, tears welling up in her eyes. "I know and I know you will be happy with me."

Franz sighed. "Are you thinking about going shopping?"

"Yes, I am about to go now." Emma confessed. She spent the next few minutes chatting with Franz about his night at the hospital before she reluctantly hung up and decided to enjoy the shopping in Paris.

Emma's day at the mall was an exercise in excess. The Champs-Élysées stretched before her like a glittering promise of escape, its high-end boutiques and luxury stores calling out to her with the seductive allure of new beginnings.

She started at Chanel, where she bought a little black dress that was anything but little in price. The soft silk fabric draped perfectly, making her feel as if she were slipping into a second skin of sophistication. Next was Louis Vuitton, where she indulged in a new handbag. The monogrammed leather was soft and supple under her fingers, a tactile reminder of the craftsmanship and status it symbolized.

At Cartier, she picked out a watch that sparkled with diamonds, a symbol of the time she was trying to reclaim. The salesperson's polished pitch about timeless elegance and eternal beauty resonated with Emma, even as she wondered if it was possible to truly buy back lost moments.

By midday, her arms were laden with bags, each one a testament to her desire to buy her way out of guilt and regret. She paused at a café, sipping on a cappuccino and watching the world go by, feeling a hollow satisfaction with her purchases. The weight of the bags was a physical reminder of her attempts to fill the void within her.

The indulgence didn't stop there. She continued her spree at Hermès, selecting a silk scarf in vibrant hues that she imagined wearing on an idyllic holiday, far from her everyday worries. At Dior, she was captivated by a pair of heels that promised to elevate not just her height but her spirits as well.

As the sun began to set, casting a golden glow over the bustling avenue, Emma made her final stop at Tiffany & Co. She chose a delicate bracelet, the tiny diamonds catching the light in a way that felt almost magical. It was a piece she hoped would symbolize new beginnings, a talisman to ward off the shadows of her past.

Emma's day at the mall, while exhilarating, also left her with a sense of unease. The fleeting joy of each purchase faded as quickly as it had come, replaced by the realization that material possessions couldn't erase the deeper issues she faced. She had spent a small fortune trying to escape her feelings, but the true cost of her spree was the acknowledgment that she needed to confront her emotions head-on.

As she made her way back to her hotel, the bags still heavy in her hands, Emma resolved to find a balance. She knew she couldn't continue using shopping as a way to fill the void. Instead, she would start looking for more meaningful ways to heal and move forward. The sparkling treasures she had acquired would serve as reminders of her journey, not just of excess but of the realization that true fulfillment comes from within.

At a chic cafe, she ordered a lavish lunch of foie gras, truffle pasta, and a glass of vintage champagne. The waiters hovered around her, attentive and polite, and she basked in their deference. She felt powerful, in control, a queen of her own little empire. But beneath the surface, the cracks were beginning to show. Her credit cards were maxed out. Emma had aspired to become a marketing maven, and now she was one. Bell Corp. hung on her every word, and she was a success making $250,000 a year.

Looking down at the empty wine glass, Emma began to think about her life outside of work. She had Franz and a few close girlfriends, but everyone else was considered an enemy or a stranger. She had worked tirelessly on the hamster wheel, and she dreamed of a day where she could get off and stretch her legs.

Emma stood before the Eiffel Tower, a monumental structure that seemed to mock her with its grandeur. Paris had progressed and moved on since her ancestors' time in France, but standing here, Emma couldn't help but feel a twinge of irony at how little things had changed in some ways.

"Ah, Paris," she mused aloud, staring up at the towering icon. "Home to romance, fashion, and the undeniable truth that even the Eiffel Tower has seen more love affairs than I've had hot dinners."

A passing couple glanced at her oddly, perhaps catching the edge of bitterness in her tone. Emma shrugged it off and continued her internal monologue, feeling the weight of history and failed romances press down on her shoulders like the tower itself.

"Here I am, staring at a symbol of modernity, wondering if my ancestors ever stood here contemplating their own absurdities," she chuckled to herself. "Probably not. They were too busy scandalizing the bourgeoisie or running off to Italy for a fling."

As tourists snapped selfies around her, Emma couldn't help but think of the absurdity of it all. The tower, once a beacon of progress and innovation, now a backdrop for Instagram feeds and overpriced souvenir shops selling miniature replicas made in China.

"Times change, Paris," she muttered, a wry smile tugging at her lips. "But some things remain constant. Like tourists flocking to the Eiffel Tower, and me, trying to make sense of it all while standing here like a lost Bovary in a sea of selfie sticks."

She turned away from the tower, shaking her head at the irony of finding universal truths in the shadows of a global icon. Paris had indeed moved on, but for Emma Bovary, some things would always remain as tangled and unattainable as the iron lattice above her.

When she got back to her hotel that afternoon, as she sat surrounded by her hauls, the realization hit her like a cold splash of water. She was living in a fantasy, a self-destructive fairy tale that was bound to end in ruin. She knew she had to change, to find a way out of the mess she had created.

Stella, however, was thrilled that Emma was having such a great time in Paris. It had been a long time since she had seen her serious daughter so lighthearted, so unburdened by the weight of her past. The transformation in Emma was palpable, and Stella felt that now would be a perfect time to introduce her to a part of her heritage that had remained hidden for too long.

Stella smiled, her eyes sparkling with excitement. "I think it's time you learned about Antoine. He was an extraordinary man, and I believe his story could bring you a sense of contentment, connection and pride."

Intrigued but wary, Emma nodded slowly. "Alright, tell me more."

Stella, a spirited woman with a knack for unearthing family secrets and spinning tales, seemed unusually excited today. Her eyes sparkled with a mischievous glint as she sipped her espresso, leaning in closer to Emma.

"Emma, I have something incredible to tell you," Stella began, her voice laced with enthusiasm. "Do you remember Antonie, my late lover who owned that magnificent estate just outside the city?"

Emma nodded, curious. Stella had often mentioned Antonie, a man of wealth and mystery whose life had been marked by opulence and grandeur.

"Well," Stella continued, "I've recently discovered something fascinating about your family history. You, my dear, have a rich ancestor."

Emma's eyes widened in surprise. It was almost as if they were on Jerry Springer and someone told her She is NOT the Mother only it sounded like this, "You ARE a rich vixen." She had always harbored a secret wish that she had some connection to a grand heritage, a lineage of wealth and sophistication that could explain her own penchant for the finer things in life.

"Are you serious, Stella?" Emma asked, her voice tinged with disbelief and excitement.

"Absolutely," Stella replied, grinning. "And there's more. Antonie's estate is now unclaimed and largely forgotten. It's a land of excess, filled with treasures and history waiting to be rediscovered. I think it's time we paid it a visit."

Emma felt a thrill run through her. The idea of exploring an estate linked to her heritage, of uncovering hidden stories and perhaps finding a deeper connection to her past, was irresistible. She felt like Stella invited her to an all-you-can-eat buffet or a diving adventure to the lost city of Atlantis.

"I can't believe this," Emma said, her mind racing with possibilities. "How did you find out about all this?"

Stella waved her hand dismissively. "Oh, you know me. I love digging into family histories and piecing together lost stories. When I realized the connection, I knew I had to tell you. So, what do you say? Shall we go see the land of excess?"

Emma hesitated for a moment, thinking of her responsibilities and the life she had built. But the pull of discovering her roots, of walking through the halls where her ancestors might have walked, was too strong to resist.

"Let's do it," she said, her voice firm with determination. "When do we leave?"

Stella's grin widened. "Tomorrow. We'll leave tomorrow morning. I've already made the arrangements."

The next day, Emma and Stella set off on their journey, their car chugging along the winding roads of the French countryside like a reluctant donkey. Emma, trying to shake off the remnants of her hangover from the previous night's escapades, squinted at the sunlit fields. The excitement between them was palpable, almost suffocatingly so, as if it were trying to force its way out of the car's air vents.

Stella, ever the enthusiastic storyteller, launched into tales of Antonie's lavish parties. "You know," she began, her eyes sparkling with mischief, "Antonie once threw a masquerade ball where everyone dressed as their favorite historical figure. The theme was 'decadent debauchery through the ages.' I heard Marie Antoinette and Julius Caesar hooked up in the wine cellar." Emma snorted, nearly veering off the road at the mental image of Julius Caesar in a powdered wig, making out with Marie Antoinette over a cask of Bordeaux.

"And the guests," Stella continued, "were legendary. The estate was graced by the likes of Picasso, Hemingway, and some Russian oligarch whose name I can't pronounce. Rumor has it they had a drinking contest with absinthe and Picasso won by painting a masterpiece while completely hammered." Emma couldn't help but laugh, imagining a drunken Picasso wielding a paintbrush like a sword, slashing colors onto a canvas in a boozy frenzy.

As the car climbed a hill, Stella lowered her voice to a conspiratorial whisper. "And then there are the whispers of hidden treasures and secret rooms. They say Antonie had a penchant for hiding things—jewels, rare artworks, incriminating letters. One time, a guest went missing during a party and was found three days later in a hidden room, completely drunk and convinced he was in a different century." Emma raised an eyebrow, pondering whether this was an adventure or an episode of "Antiques Roadshow: After Dark."

Stella's stories wove a tapestry of eccentricity and opulence, and Emma's mind spun with the possibilities. "So, basically," she said, "we're driving into a Scooby-Doo episode where the ghosts are replaced by the drunken ghosts of artists and writers." Stella laughed, nodding enthusiastically. "Exactly! Except instead of unmasking the villain, we might unearth a treasure chest or a secret love letter."

The countryside whizzed by, a blur of green and gold, as Stella continued her tales. "I heard there's a secret passage that leads from the library to the wine cellar. Perfect for a quick escape or a midnight snack, depending on your priorities." Emma chuckled, imagining herself in a dramatic escape, dodging imaginary laser beams with a baguette in one hand and a bottle of vintage wine in the other.

As they approached the estate, an imposing silhouette on the horizon, Emma's excitement mingled with a healthy dose of skepticism. The stories were grand, but she half-expected to find a dilapidated mansion with more cobwebs than chandeliers. "Well, Stella," she said, gripping the steering wheel, "if we don't find hidden treasures, at least we'll have a great story to tell."

Stella grinned, her eyes twinkling with anticipation. "Oh, Emma, I have a feeling this trip is going to be legendary, one way or another." They pulled up to the grand gates of the estate, which creaked open ominously, as if welcoming them into a world where reality and legend blurred in the most delightfully absurd ways.

When they finally arrived at the estate, Emma was awestruck. The grand mansion, though weathered by time, still exuded an air of elegance and opulence. Ivy crawled up the stone walls, and the gardens, though overgrown, hinted at their former glory. Stella led Emma through the main gates and into the grand foyer, where a massive chandelier hung from the ceiling, sparkling with dust-covered crystals. The air was thick with history, and Emma could almost hear the echoes of the past – the laughter of guests, the clinking of glasses, and the soft strains of music.

As they explored room after room, each filled with antiques and artifacts, Emma felt a deep sense of connection. She imagined her ancestors walking these halls, living their lives in a world of elegance and sophistication. The experience was both humbling and exhilarating.

Emma and Stella stood at the entrance of Antonie's sprawling estate, feeling like fish out of water in a sea of decadence. The sheer size of the mansion was enough to make their jaws drop, but it was the ostentatious decor that truly caught them off guard.

"Stella, this place is... it's like a museum on steroids," Emma muttered under her breath, trying to process the grandeur before her.

Stella chuckled, her eyes wide with amusement. "I know, right? I feel like we've stepped into a movie set where everyone is trying too hard."

They ventured cautiously into the foyer, where a life-sized marble statue of a Greek god greeted them with a stern expression. Emma couldn't help but snort softly at the sight. "Do you think they have a matching goddess for balance?"

Stella stifled a laugh, nodding towards a hallway lined with gilded frames and imposing portraits. "I bet these are all ancestors who were probably just as pretentious."

As they wandered deeper into the mansion, every room seemed to outdo the last in extravagance. The dining room boasted a chandelier that could rival the sun in brightness, while the sitting room was filled with antique furniture that looked more like props from a historical drama.

"I feel like we need to whisper in case we disturb the delicate balance of absurdity," Emma joked, glancing at a gold-plated piano in the corner.

Stella nodded in agreement, her voice low as if in a conspiracy. "Do you think they polish the gold every day or just on weekends?"

They paused in front of a particularly ornate mirror, its frame adorned with intricate carvings of cherubs and vines. Emma couldn't resist making faces at her reflection, causing Stella to burst into quiet giggles beside her.

"I'm not sure I can ever get used to this," Emma admitted, shaking her head in disbelief. "I mean, who needs this much gold leaf in their life?"

Stella smirked, her eyes twinkling mischievously. "Maybe we should take some home as a souvenir. I hear gold leaf makes a great conversation starter."

Emma laughed, feeling lighter despite the overwhelming surroundings. "Can you imagine? 'Oh, this old thing? Just picked it up at Antonie's place.'"

Their tour through the mansion continued, each room offering new wonders and absurdities. Despite feeling like two mismatched puzzle pieces in a world of perfectly fitted elegance, Emma and Stella found humor in their discomfort. In the library, Stella handed Emma an old leather-bound journal. "I found this among Antonie's things. It belonged to your great-great-grandfather. I thought you might like to have it."

Emma took the journal, her fingers tracing the worn cover. She opened it carefully, her eyes scanning the elegant script of her ancestor's words. It was a window into the past, a glimpse of the life he had led and the legacy he had left behind.

"Thank you, Stella," Emma said, her voice filled with gratitude. "This means more to me than you could ever know."

Emma felt a lump in her throat as she looked around. The weight of her heritage pressed down on her, but it was not an oppressive burden. Instead, it felt like a mantle of strength, a reminder that she was part of something much larger than herself.

Stella guided her through the rooms, sharing stories of Antoine's life, his struggles, and his triumphs. Emma listened, captivated, feeling a deep connection to this man she had never known. As they walked through the library, filled with leather-bound books and ancient manuscripts, she felt a sense of belonging she had never experienced before.

"Stella," Emma said softly, "thank you for bringing me here. I feel like I've discovered a part of myself I didn't know existed."

Stella smiled, her eyes warm with affection. "You are a remarkable woman, Emma. Antoine's blood runs in your veins, and his spirit lives on in you. Embrace your heritage and let it guide you."

That evening, as they sat by the fireplace, Emma felt a profound sense of peace. The anger, shame, and regret from her past seemed to melt away, replaced by a newfound resolve. But now, she saw a different path, one where she could honor her heritage and build a future that made her proud.

In the quiet moments of that night, Emma made a promise to herself. She would continue to be financially responsible, to work hard and live within her means. She would cherish her family's legacy and strive to be the best version of herself. And most importantly, she would let go of the past and embrace the future with courage and grace.

Stella took Emma's hand, leading her through the quaint, cobblestone streets of Colmar. The picturesque town, with its timber-framed houses and vibrant flower boxes, seemed like something out of a fairy tale. Emma, accustomed to the bustling energy of Brooklyn, felt a surreal calm wash over her. The journey had been long, but the destination promised something extraordinary.

"This is all yours," Stella said, her voice brimming with a Vanna White charm as she gestured expansively. Emma's mouth dropped open, her eyes wide with disbelief. She felt like she had just stepped into a game show or a movie, where the impossible suddenly became reality.

As she stood there, taking it all in, Emma felt like the protagonist in a story that was only just beginning. The mansion, the servants, the vault of money—everything was hers, and she was ready to step into this new chapter with a sense of wonder and anticipation. The world outside seemed far away, and for the first time, Emma felt a sense of belonging, a certainty that she was exactly where she was meant to be.

As Emma stood in the vault, surrounded by the symbols of her newfound wealth, a swirl of thoughts enveloped her mind. The magnitude of her inheritance was overwhelming, but amidst the shock and excitement, a clear realization began to crystallize.

Franz.

Her mind raced to him—Franz, her kind and brilliant husband, tirelessly working long hours at the hospital. He had always been there for her, supporting her dreams even when they seemed far-fetched. How could she ever repay him for his unwavering dedication and love?

At that moment, Emma knew she had to stop working for other people. This wealth was an opportunity—a chance to reshape her life and, by extension, Franz's. She needed to harness this fortune, not just for herself, but to create something meaningful, something that could also help Franz. Perhaps a foundation or a clinic, a way to merge their passions and create lasting change.

Emma's mind buzzed with possibilities. She imagined starting her own business, investing in projects that excited her, and, most importantly, freeing Franz from the grueling demands of his job. With their combined talents and resources, they could build something remarkable together.

She could almost see Franz's reaction in her mind's eye—his shock, his joy, the disbelief slowly transforming into a radiant smile. He was going to die when she told him the news. The thought brought a smile to her lips, and for the first time in a long while, Emma felt a profound sense of purpose and direction.

"Stella," Emma said, her voice steady but soft, "I think it's time for me to go home."

Stella looked at her, a knowing smile playing at the corners of her lips. "I understand, Emma. You've been through a lot, and it's time to take all this and make it yours. Let's not waste any time, then. I am satisfied, I outlived Antonie and Marguerite. Talk about a homerun." She laughed out loud.

Emma and Stella made their way to the private airstrip. The path was overgrown with weeds, and the once-grand statues lining the way were now draped in vines, their expressions appearing more exasperated than ever. The sleek jet waiting at the end of the path was a stark contrast to the dilapidation surrounding it, like a diamond in a pile of rubble.

"Ah, the good ol' days of wealth and excess," Stella said, a wry smile playing on her lips. "I always wondered what it would be like to have a personal jet. Turns out, it's a lot like having a really expensive car you never use. All show, no practicality."

Emma chuckled, her mood lightened by Stella's humor. "Well, at least we're not taking a horse-drawn carriage. Can you imagine the looks we'd get pulling up to the airport in that?"

They boarded the jet, the plush leather seats and champagne flutes mocking the decrepitude they left behind. As the engines roared to life, Stella leaned back, sipping her champagne. "You know, I always wanted to live like the rich and famous. Now I realize, they just spend more money to be just as miserable as the rest of us."

Emma raised her glass in a toast. "To being fabulously miserable, then."

The jet ascended, and the estate quickly became a small dot in the landscape below. Emma looked out the window, feeling a strange mix of elation and melancholy. The journey from the opulence of the estate to the simplicity of home felt symbolic, as if she were shedding an old skin to reveal something new underneath.

"So, how does it feel to know you have a rich ancestor?" Stella asked, breaking the silence.

Emma shrugged. "Like discovering the Monopoly man is my great-uncle."

Stella laughed, her eyes twinkling. "I talked to an accountant and lawyer of the trust. If we liquidate it all, it will be worth $1.3 billion."

As they neared their destination, the city lights twinkling below, Emma felt a sense of closure. The past, with all its secrets and excesses, had been a strange but enlightening adventure. Now, she was ready to face her future, armed with the knowledge of where she came from and a large sum of money. She knew she could overcome even the temptations to be with a hunk like Leon.

As the jet soared above the clouds, Emma sat back in her plush seat, feeling the hum of the engines beneath her. The world below was a patchwork quilt of greens and blues, fading into the vast horizon. She placed her hand on her belly, absentmindedly tracing circles, when she felt a strange fluttering sensation. A sudden, gentle kick made her eyes widen in realization. She was pregnant.

The news filled her with a mixture of joy and wonder, adding another layer of excitement and anticipation to the already transformative day. It was as if the universe had decided to give her the ultimate surprise, a precious gift nestled within her, waiting to be revealed.

Emma's thoughts raced. She had always dreamed of becoming a mother, but the timing of this revelation felt like the final piece of a puzzle falling into place. Her journey to Colmar, the anticipation of seeing the huge estate that awaited her, and now this—a new life growing inside her. It was almost too much to take in.

She glanced out the window, watching the cotton-candy clouds drift by, and allowed herself to bask in the moment. The future seemed bright, filled with endless possibilities. She imagined holding her baby for the first time, the warmth and softness of tiny fingers wrapping around hers. She pictured late-night feedings, the smell of baby powder, and the sweet sound of giggles filling her home.

The flight attendant appeared beside her, offering a warm smile. "Can I get you anything, ma'am?"

Emma shook her head, returning the smile. "No, thank you. I'm just... enjoying the view."

The attendant nodded and moved on, leaving Emma to her thoughts. She leaned back and closed her eyes, letting the rhythmic thrum of the engines lull her into a peaceful state. Her mind wandered to Franz. How would he react to the news? She hoped he would be as thrilled as she was. They had their ups and downs, but this baby could be the glue that held them together, a fresh start for their family.

Emma's hand rested on her belly, where she felt another tiny kick. She smiled, feeling a deep sense of connection to the life growing within her. It was a reminder of the strength and resilience she possessed, of her ability to create and nurture something beautiful.

On the plane a palatial idea came to Emma. She would help Franz further his career with the money she had inherited. He knew better than anyone how the medical community could use a boost in funding. Perhaps, she could talk him into using it for epilepsy research, she mused. He was going to be thrilled.

When the jet began its descent, Emma's thoughts turned again to Franz. She could hardly wait to share the news with him, not just about the inheritance, but about their future child. The jet touched down smoothly, and as it taxied to a stop, she spotted Franz waiting eagerly by the runway, his eyes scanning the plane with a mix of confusion and curiosity.

The door of the jet opened, and Emma stepped out, her heart racing. Franz's eyes widened in shock as he took in the scene. "What the heck is this?" he exclaimed, his voice a mix of disbelief and irritation.

Emma raised a hand, trying to calm him. "Franz, please, let me explain—"

But Stella interjected, stepping forward with a stern expression. "Now, yelling at your beautiful wife is quite the faux pas, is it not?" Her words cut through the tension, causing Franz to blink and collect himself.

Franz took a deep breath, his shoulders relaxing slightly. "I'm sorry, Emma. It's just... this is a lot to take in."

Emma smiled gently, reaching out to take his hand. "I know, and I promise I'll explain everything. Come on, let's talk in the car."

A sleek black Phantom awaited them, its polished exterior gleaming in the sunlight. They climbed into the luxurious vehicle, and as it pulled away from the airport, Emma began to recount the incredible events of the past few days. She told Franz about the estate, the inheritance, and finally, about the baby.

Franz listened in stunned silence, his eyes wide with amazement. When she finished, he reached over and took her hand, squeezing it gently. "Emma, this is... unbelievable. I don't even know what to say."

Emma leaned against him, feeling a sense of relief wash over her. "Just say you'll be with me, every step of the way."

Franz smiled, his eyes shining with love and determination. "Always, Emma. Always."

Emma was determined to show Franz just how much he meant to her. He had been her rock, her confidant, and now the father of her unborn child. As a world-renowned surgeon, Franz was often burdened with the weight of his responsibilities, and Emma wanted to give him the relaxed, uncomplicated life he deserved—wrapped in the finest luxuries.

Her first gift was a handcrafted leather briefcase, elegant and sophisticated. "For carrying all your important documents in style," she said, placing a soft kiss on his cheek. "Every time you pick it up, I want you to remember how much I love you and how proud I am of everything you do."

Next, she arranged a surprise getaway to a private villa in the Italian countryside. Franz had always wanted to visit Tuscany, but his busy schedule had never allowed for it. The drive to the villa was picturesque, winding through the lush green hills of Tuscany, dotted with cypress trees and sun-drenched vineyards. Emma and Franz's anticipation grew with each turn. When they finally arrived, the villa stood as a beacon of tranquility, an old stone building surrounded by blooming lavender and olive trees.

"Welcome to your sanctuary," Emma said, her voice soft but filled with excitement.

Franz looked around in awe. "It's perfect," he murmured, his eyes wide with wonder.

They stepped inside, greeted by rustic charm and modern comforts. The air was fragrant with the scent of fresh flowers and the rich aroma of Italian cuisine wafting from the kitchen.

"I've arranged for a private chef," Emma said, leading Franz through the rooms. "So you can truly relax and enjoy every moment."

They made their way to the terrace, which offered a breathtaking view of the rolling vineyards below. The sun was setting, casting a warm, golden glow over the landscape. Emma slipped her arms around Franz's waist, her touch gentle yet possessive.

"This place is our sanctuary," she whispered, her lips brushing against his ear. "A place where you can escape from the chaos of the world and just be."

Franz turned to face her, his eyes filled with gratitude and love. "You always know exactly what I need," he said, pulling her close.

The evening progressed with a lavish dinner, featuring locally sourced ingredients and exquisite wines. They laughed and talked, savoring each bite and each other's company. As the night grew darker, the terrace was illuminated by soft candlelight, creating an intimate, almost magical atmosphere.

Emma led Franz to the master bedroom, which was adorned with silk sheets and scattered rose petals. "I thought we could make the most of this beautiful place," she said, a mischievous glint in her eye.

Franz grinned, his earlier awe transforming into a more primal hunger. "I like the way you think."

They undressed slowly, savoring the anticipation. The room was filled with the scent of lavender and the soft sounds of the Italian countryside. Emma's fingers traced the contours of Franz's body, each touch igniting a spark of desire.

As they lay down on the bed, the silk sheets cool against their skin, Franz pulled Emma close, his lips capturing hers in a passionate kiss.

Their bodies moved together, a dance of desire and love, each touch and caress building the intensity between them.

"You're my sanctuary," Franz whispered against her skin, his voice thick with emotion.

Emma's laughter was soft and breathless. "And you're my escape," she replied, her hands exploring the familiar terrain of his body.

Their lovemaking was a mix of tender intimacy and raw passion. Emma arched beneath Franz, her nails digging into his back as he moved within her, their rhythm perfect and unhurried. They lost themselves in the moment, their connection deepening with each passing second.

Afterward, they lay tangled in the sheets, their breathing gradually slowing. Franz brushed a lock of hair from Emma's face, his touch tender. "Thank you for this," he said softly. "For everything."

Emma smiled, her heart full. "I wanted to give you something special. A place where we can just be ourselves."

"You've given me more than that," Franz said, his voice choked with emotion. "You've given me a reason to believe in happiness again."

They spent the next few days exploring the countryside, tasting local wines, and reveling in the simple pleasures of life. The villa became their haven, a place where they could escape from the pressures of the outside world and simply enjoy each other's company.

As their stay came to an end, Franz stood on the terrace, looking out over the vineyards one last time. Emma came up behind him, slipping her arms around his waist.

"I think this place has worked its magic," Franz said, his voice soft.

Emma nodded, resting her head on his shoulder. "It's our sanctuary, Franz. A place where we can always come back to, no matter what."

Franz turned to face her, his eyes filled with love and gratitude. "You've made my dreams come true, Emma."

"And you've made mine," she replied, her lips meeting his in a kiss filled with promise and hope.

Franz's eyes lit up with gratitude and joy, and they spent the week exploring the local culture, enjoying wine tastings, and indulging in gourmet meals. But Emma's surprises didn't stop there. She had meticulously planned each detail to ensure Franz felt pampered and cherished.

In the evenings, she would draw a warm bath infused with fragrant essential oils, lighting candles around the room to create a soothing ambiance. "You deserve to unwind," she would say, gently guiding him into the tub. She would sit beside him, massaging his shoulders, and whispering sweet nothings in his ear.

One night, after a particularly relaxing bath, Emma led Franz to their bedroom. She had transformed it into a haven of romance—silk sheets, soft music playing in the background, and rose petals scattered across the bed. She had bought him a luxurious silk robe, which she helped him into after their bath.

"This robe is for when you need to feel completely at ease," she said, running her hands over the smooth fabric. "I want you to always feel the comfort and love that surrounds you."

Emma took great pleasure in spoiling Franz in the bedroom. She would take her time, making sure he felt adored and appreciated. She would kiss every inch of his body, her lips moving slowly and deliberately. "You deserve all the pleasure in the world," she would murmur, her voice husky with desire.

She bought him high-quality, tailored pajamas, saying, "For the man who saves lives, the least he can have is the finest sleepwear." She would then lead him to bed, ensuring he felt completely relaxed and cared for.

On their anniversary, Emma gifted Franz a custom-made watch, engraved with the words, "For every second we spend together." She handed it to him during a candlelit dinner at home, a feast she had prepared with all his favorite dishes. "This is a reminder that no matter where you are, I'm always thinking of you."

Franz was overwhelmed by her thoughtfulness and devotion. He pulled her close, his voice filled with emotion. "Emma, you make me feel like the luckiest man alive. You've given me more than I could ever ask for."

Emma smiled, brushing her lips against his. "You deserve everything, Franz. And I'll spend my life making sure you have it."

In their intimate moments, Emma was attentive and affectionate, always putting Franz's needs and desires first. She would often initiate their lovemaking with a sensual massage, her hands working out the tension in his muscles. "I want you to feel completely at ease," she would whisper, her breath warm against his skin.

Their nights together were filled with passion and tenderness. Emma took her time, exploring his body with a loving touch, always making sure he felt cherished and adored. She delighted in seeing the pleasure in his eyes, knowing she was giving him the love and care he so deeply deserved.

As they lay together afterwards, Emma would often trace patterns on his chest, her fingers moving lazily over his skin. "I love you, Franz," she would say, her voice soft and sincere. "And I will always make sure you know just how much."

Franz would smile, pulling her close and kissing her forehead. "I love you too, Emma. You've given me a life I never even dreamed was possible."

Part 4

In Brooklyn's bustling streets, Emma strides with grace, A warrior's spirit, a beacon in the race. Her path unfolds with faith's gentle embrace, Guided by love, surrounded by grace.
Converted to Catholicism's calming fold, Emma finds solace in stories long told. Her mother's faith, a beacon bright and bold, Guides her steps, as her story's told.
In every corner, in every heartfelt deed, She plants seeds of hope, where souls find need. Her mother's prayers, a gentle, quiet creed, In Emma's legacy, love's eternal seed.
No longer bound by boardroom's stern demands, She walks serenely through Brooklyn's busy strands. A legacy unfolds, not in gold or fame, But in the gentle grace of Emma's name.
With each kind word and every thoughtful deed, She plants seeds of love, where hearts find heed. In Emma's legacy, the city finds its peace, A testament to love that will never cease.
For Emma's child, a future bright, Guided by her love, a shining light, In every moment, a mother's embrace, Emma's legacy, in time and space.
Emma had never anticipated that loving Franz would be so challenging. It wasn't because of any flaw in him; Franz was kind, attentive, and understanding. Rather, the difficulty lay within herself, a battle with shadows from her past and fears of her own nature. Every day, she wrestled with the disquieting similarities between herself and Madame Bovary, a character who had once fascinated and terrified her. She had first encountered Emma Bovary during a reading session after her

wedding. Now, a year later, those echoes returned, haunting her as she navigated her life with Franz. She feared that this discontent could lead her down a similar path of dissatisfaction and recklessness, jeopardizing the very happiness she so cherished with Franz.

To combat these fears, Emma made a conscious effort to become a better version of herself. She immersed herself in self-reflection and sought ways to ground her restless spirit. She began attending Mass with Franz, drawn to the rituals and the sense of community within the Catholic Church. Though she had never been particularly religious, she found solace in the structure and the teachings that offered a different perspective on her life and choices.

The decision to convert to Catholicism was not made lightly. It was a journey fraught with doubts and inner conflict. Yet, as she delved deeper into her new faith, Emma discovered a profound sense of peace and purpose. The Church's emphasis on vocation and duty provided her with a framework to channel her energies in a meaningful way.

She began to see her role as Franz's wife through the lens of her faith. Caring for him was not just a matter of personal fulfillment but a sacred duty. This shift in perspective helped Emma to appreciate the small, everyday moments they shared—preparing meals together, long walks in the park, and quiet evenings reading by the fireplace. These were not just mundane activities but expressions of her commitment and love.

Despite her newfound clarity, the shadows of Madame Bovary lingered. There were days when Emma felt the old restlessness rising within her, the desire to escape into a world of excitement and novelty. But now, she recognized these feelings as part of her past self, remainders of a life she no longer wanted to lead. Instead of succumbing to these impulses, she used them as opportunities to reaffirm her commitment to Franz and her faith.

Emma threw herself into her new role with a dedication that surprised even her. She found joy in the simple acts of service—cooking

Franz's favorite meals, keeping their home warm and inviting, and supporting him in his work. She volunteered at their parish, finding fulfillment in helping others and contributing to their community.

Her relationship with Franz grew stronger with each passing day. They faced challenges and obstacles, but their shared faith and mutual commitment provided a solid foundation. Emma no longer saw herself in the tragic light of Madame Bovary. Instead, she saw herself as a woman who had faced her fears and emerged stronger, with a deeper understanding of love and duty.

One evening, as they sat together on their porch watching the sunset, Franz took her hand in his. "I've noticed a change in you, Emma," he said softly. "You seem more at peace."

Emma smiled, feeling a warmth spread through her. "I think I've finally found my path, Franz. Being with you, caring for you—it's become my vocation. And I wouldn't trade it for anything."

Franz squeezed her hand, his eyes filled with love. "I'm so grateful for you, Emma. You bring so much light into my life. You are irreplaceable."

Emma sat alone in the dim light of her study, a solitary figure amidst the encroaching shadows. The house was quiet, the silence punctuated only by the ticking of the old grandfather clock in the hall. Yes, it was gilded and bougie as hell, but she loved it. Her Grandma Stella loved it, too. She had spent countless nights like this, lost in thought, grappling with a sense of restlessness that had plagued her for as long as she could remember.

Her grandmother's faith had been a constant, unwavering presence, a source of strength and comfort in times of trouble. Emma had long since drifted away from those early teachings, caught up in the whirlwind of life, ambition, and an insatiable desire for excitement. But now, as she sat in the quiet of her study, the weight of her choices pressed heavily upon her. She realized, with a clarity that startled her, that the very qualities she admired in her grandmother—her resilience, her grace, her unwavering sense of purpose—were rooted in the faith she had so casually discarded.

The realization was a painful one. It brought with it a deep sense of loss, a recognition of the years spent chasing after fleeting pleasures and empty promises. Emma felt as if she had been running in circles, always seeking something just out of reach, never realizing that what she truly needed had been there all along.

Emma began to attend Mass regularly, immersing herself in the teachings of the Church. She sought guidance from the priest, who listened with kindness and offered counsel. She joined a study group, where she met others who were also seeking to deepen their faith. Slowly, gradually, she began to feel a change within herself. The decision to convert was not without its challenges. There were moments of doubt and uncertainty, times when she questioned whether she was truly worthy of this new path. But through it all, Emma found solace in prayer and in the community of believers who surrounded her with support and encouragement.

Emma's newfound faith brought a sense of perspective and clarity that she had never experienced before. She learned to appreciate the simple, everyday moments—the joy of a shared meal, the comfort of a quiet evening together, the satisfaction of caring for their home and for each other. These were not just tasks to be completed but acts of love and devotion.

As Emma's transformation unfolded, the women of SoHo began to take notice. They were a diverse group, connected through a shared sense of community and curiosity about the world around them. Some were descendants of Emma's great-grandmother's fashion customers, while others were the daughters of the neighborhood's nosy ladies, and still more were new neighbors looking to connect.

It started with casual nods and smiles exchanged in passing on the bustling streets of SoHo. Emma would often find herself greeted warmly at the local coffee shop, where conversations about art, literature, and current events would naturally unfold. She felt a sense of belonging as invitations to gatherings and events started coming her way.

One sunny afternoon, as she walked down Greene Street, Emma was approached by Claire, a vibrant woman in her fifties who owned a boutique nearby. "Emma, darling, you simply must join us for brunch this weekend," Claire insisted with a friendly smile. "The ladies would love to get to know you better. We've heard so much about your recent endeavors!"

Emma hesitated at first, still adjusting to this newfound attention and acceptance. But Claire's warmth was infectious, and she found herself agreeing. Soon, she was attending art gallery openings, charity fundraisers, and neighborhood picnics, surrounded by women of all ages and backgrounds who welcomed her into their circle.

At these gatherings, Emma discovered a rich tapestry of stories and experiences. She bonded over shared interests in fashion and design with women who remembered her great-grandmother's elegant dresses. She exchanged ideas about community engagement and social justice with the daughters of the neighborhood's longtime residents. And she connected with new neighbors who were eager to explore SoHo's vibrant culture alongside her.

Through these interactions, Emma felt her sense of purpose deepen. She realized that her journey of self-discovery wasn't just about personal growth—it was about forging meaningful connections and contributing to the fabric of her community. She embraced the opportunity to learn from the women around her, drawing inspiration from their resilience, creativity, and passion for making a difference.

As the days turned into weeks and months, Emma's circle of friends in SoHo grew stronger. She found herself surrounded by a supportive network of women who celebrated her transformation and encouraged her to continue pursuing her dreams. Together, they embarked on new adventures, shared laughter and tears, and created lasting memories that would shape Emma's journey for years to come.

In the heart of SoHo, amidst the bustling streets and eclectic storefronts, Emma had found not only her true self but also a community that welcomed her with open arms—a community where she could thrive, contribute, and grow into the woman she had always aspired to be.

One evening, as Emma knelt in prayer, she felt a profound sense of gratitude. She thanked God for the journey that had led her back to her faith, for the pain and suffering that had been the catalyst for her transformation. She understood now that her mother's faith had been the source of her uniqueness, the wellspring of her strength and grace.

The only way to Franz's heart was by being authentic, genuine, and a decent person. This realization struck Emma with a force that left her breathless. Could she truly transform herself? Could she one-up her own nature, shedding the layers of restlessness and discontent that had once defined her?

As she attended Mass and prayed, Emma thought often of Charles. The character of Charles Bovary had been the epitome of simplicity and decency, yet Emma Bovary had seen him as nothing more than a tool to achieve her own ends. Emma vowed not to repeat the same mistakes. She wanted her relationship with Franz to be built on mutual respect and genuine affection, not on manipulation and deceit.

One evening, after a particularly moving sermon, Emma sat with Franz in the quiet of their home. She looked into his eyes, searching for the words to express the profound changes taking place within her.

"Franz," she began, her voice trembling slightly, "I've been doing a lot of thinking. About us, about my faith, about who I want to be."

Franz listened, his expression open and encouraging. "Tell me, Emma. I'm here for you."

She took a deep breath, gathering her thoughts. "I don't want to be like Emma Bovary. I don't want to use people or manipulate them to get what I want. I want our relationship to be different—honest, real, and pure. I want to be a better person, for you and for myself."

Franz reached out, taking her hand in his. "I see the changes in you, Emma. I see your dedication, your sincerity. You've always had a good heart, but now, it's shining even brighter."

His words filled her with warmth and determination. Emma realized that the path to Franz's heart was not through grand gestures or calculated moves but through the simple, everyday acts of kindness and love. She focused on being present in the moment, appreciating the beauty of their life together and finding joy in the small things.

She found herself drawing closer to Franz, their bond growing stronger with each passing day. They prayed together, shared their hopes and dreams, and supported each other in their spiritual journeys. Emma's newfound faith provided a foundation for their relationship, grounding it in values that transcended the fleeting desires and whims that had once consumed her.

One night, as they sat together on their porch, watching the stars twinkle in the night sky, Emma turned to Franz and smiled. "I feel like I'm finally becoming the person I was meant to be," she said softly.

Franz wrapped his arm around her, pulling her close. "You've always been that person, Emma. It just took a little time for you to see it. Your Grandma Stella did an excellent job." He cuddled her close, and for the first time, she felt truly seen and appreciated. In his embrace, Emma felt a profound sense of peace.

Franz found himself inspired by her dedication and inner strength. He realized that if he didn't grow and become more dynamic, he risked losing the woman who had become the center of his world. Franz was haunted by the cautionary tale of Charles Bovary. Charles had been devastated by Emma Bovary's affairs, ultimately succumbing to a life of bitterness and poverty. Without Emma around, Charles had been unable to rule even himself, his heart hardened and his spirit broken. Franz knew he did not want to meet the same fate. He wanted to be a man worthy of Emma's love, a partner who could stand beside her with strength and integrity.

Inspired by Emma's change and commitment to virtue, Franz found himself at a crossroads. Her transformation had stirred something deep within him, igniting a desire to become a better version of himself. He began by reassessing his priorities, understanding that to match Emma's newfound serenity and purpose, he needed to embark on a journey of personal growth and self-improvement.

Franz started with his career. He realized that true success required more than just getting by—it demanded passion, innovation, and dedication. He began to take on new challenges at work, seeking out projects that pushed his boundaries and allowed him to explore uncharted territories.

Beyond his professional life, Franz also focused on personal development. He began reading voraciously, diving into books on leadership, psychology, and self-improvement. He attended seminars and workshops, eager to learn from experts and peers. He sought out mentors who could provide guidance and insight, helping him navigate the complexities of his new role and his evolving identity.

Franz also made a concerted effort to improve his physical health. He started exercising regularly, incorporating a mix of cardio, strength training, and yoga into his routine. He adjusted his diet, opting for nutritious, balanced meals that fueled his body and mind. The physical changes were apparent—he felt stronger, more energetic, and more confident.

Emma noticed the difference. She saw the spark in Franz's eyes, the determination in his stride, and the joy he took in his accomplishments. They often discussed their journeys over dinner, sharing insights and supporting each other's growth. Emma was proud of Franz, and her admiration only fueled his drive to keep pushing forward.

Their relationship deepened as they navigated these changes together. They found new ways to connect, whether it was through a shared hobby, like hiking, or simply spending quiet evenings at home, talking about their dreams and aspirations. Franz's commitment to virtue and personal growth brought a new dimension to their bond, one that was built on mutual respect and a shared vision for the future.

One evening, as they sat on the terrace of their home, looking out at the city lights, Franz took Emma's hand. "You've inspired me more than you'll ever know," he said softly. "Because of you, I've found a part of myself that I didn't even know existed."

Emma smiled, squeezing his hand. "And because of you, I've learned what it means to truly love and be loved. Together, we can achieve anything."

Franz nodded, feeling a profound sense of gratitude. He knew that his journey was far from over, but with Emma by his side, he was ready to face whatever challenges lay ahead. His life had taken on new meaning, one that was rich with purpose, growth, and love.

As Franz continued to excel in his career and personal life, his success became a testament to the power of transformation and commitment to virtue. He became a role model for others, inspiring colleagues, friends, and even strangers with his story. As Franz grew in his professional life, he also worked on his personal development. He became more attentive and supportive, striving to be the best husband he could be. He and Emma spent more time together, deepening their bond through shared experiences and mutual respect. Their relationship flourished, built on a foundation of love, faith, and genuine commitment to each other's well-being.

Their love story took a new and joyful turn when Emma gave birth to their daughter, Clara. The arrival of their child brought immense happiness and a renewed sense of purpose. They were determined to raise Clara in a stable and loving environment, providing her with the security and opportunities they had both longed for in their own lives.

One sunny afternoon, as Emma and Franz sat on their porch watching Clara play in the garden, they reflected on the path that had led them here. Emma turned to Franz, her eyes filled with gratitude and love.

"We've come so far, haven't we?" she said softly. "I'm so thankful for you and for the life we've built together."

Franz squeezed her hand, his eyes shining with affection. "I couldn't have done it without you, Emma. You've inspired me to be a better man, and I'm grateful for every moment we've shared."

Emma smiled, feeling a deep sense of peace. She knew that their journey was far from over, but she was ready to face whatever challenges lay ahead, secure in the knowledge that they would face them together. Their love had been tested and refined by adversity, and it had emerged stronger and more resilient.

Stella's death was a turning point in Emma's life, a moment of profound sorrow and a catalyst for deep introspection. Stella had always been a beacon of light and wisdom, but as her health declined, she became increasingly reflective. On her final day, she looked at Emma with a serene smile, whispering, "I must go before I become Homais himself." Her chuckle was soft, almost whimsical, as she closed her eyes and drifted into a deep sleep.

Emma was left to grapple with the loss, a void that seemed impossible to fill. Yet, she knew she had to move forward, not just for herself but for the life she was carrying within her. Emma found herself compelled to understand the enigmatic reference Stella had made. Homais was a symbol of mediocrity and complacency. Stella's words, cryptic yet meaningful, pushed Emma to ensure her life did not mirror the tragic flaws of the past.

For Franz, learning to trust Emma was both a challenge and a necessity. His family's history had been marked by turmoil and hardship, particularly during the Normandy crisis. They had lived through the devastation and chaos, and Franz had grown up with stories of resilience and survival. Franz's grandfather was one of the soldier's who stormed the beach in Normandy. He was lucky enough to make it to safety and took refuge in Yonville, where the allure and dramatic demise of the aristocrat Emma Bovary was still talked about in certain circles. Franz's ancestor ended up succumbing to his injuries but not before he was able to write home about what he had found in Yonville. The name Emma Bovary had been a part of those tales, an intriguing person whose actions had led to ruin.

Franz's family had grown up knowing who Emma Bovary was. When Franz first met Emma at one of his epilepsy talks, her name sounded eerily familiar. Yet, it wasn't just her name that captivated him; it was her presence, her strength, and the aura of transformation that surrounded her.

At first, Franz was wary. The echoes of Emma Bovary's legacy haunted him, making him cautious about opening his heart. But as he got to know Emma, he saw the stark differences between her and the tragic figure from her family's past. Emma was genuine, sincere, and deeply committed to becoming a better person.

Franz recalled their first conversation at the talk. Emma had approached him with a mixture of curiosity and humility, eager to learn more about his work and share her own journey. Her openness and honesty struck a chord with him, and he found himself drawn to her in ways he hadn't expected.

"I've heard your name before," Franz had said cautiously, trying to gauge her reaction.

Emma smiled, a hint of sadness in her eyes. "Yes, Emma Bovary. I know the story well. But I am not her, Franz. I've learned from my past, and I'm committed to a different future."

Her words resonated with him, and slowly, Franz began to lower his defenses. He saw the sincerity in her actions, the way she cared for others, and her unwavering commitment to their relationship. Over time, trust blossomed between them, replacing the initial wariness with a deep and abiding love.

One sunny afternoon, as Emma and Franz sat on their balcony watching Clara play in the garden, they reflected on the path that had led them here. Emma turned to Franz, her eyes filled with gratitude and love.

"We've come so far, haven't we?" she said softly. "I'm so thankful for you and for the life we've built together."

Alright, so let's talk about the rest of our lives," Emma said, leaning back in her chair with a playful smirk. "No pressure or anything."

Franz chuckled, reaching over to take her hand. "Sure, just a casual conversation about our entire future. Piece of cake."

They both laughed, the sound mingling with the distant city noise. But beneath the humor was a shared sense of purpose and excitement. They had both come a long way, and now they were ready to build something even greater together.

"First things first," Emma began, "we need to diversify our investments. I was thinking about putting some money into crypto. It's risky, but the potential returns are huge."

Franz nodded thoughtfully. "Crypto is a rollercoaster, but you're right. We can afford to take some risks. Besides, I hear Bitcoin is the new gold."

Emma rolled her eyes with a grin. "Oh please, don't start with the tech-bro lingo. But seriously, we should get a financial advisor to help us navigate that world."

"Agreed," Franz said, lifting his glass in a mock toast. "To becoming crypto millionaires."

Emma clinked her glass against his, then continued. "Next, real estate. We've talked about buying a property upstate. Somewhere we can escape to on weekends, a place for the kids to play and for us to relax."

Franz's eyes lit up. "Yes! A big house with lots of land. Maybe near a lake or with a view of the mountains. We can teach the kids to fish, hike, and appreciate nature. It sounds perfect."

"Perfectly expensive," Emma teased. "But worth it. Speaking of the kids, we need to think about their education. Private schools, the best tutors, everything they need to succeed."

Franz squeezed her hand. "Absolutely. Our children deserve the best start in life. We'll find a school that values creativity and critical thinking, not just rote learning. And maybe some classes on how to deal with having parents who invest in crypto."

Emma laughed. "They'll need all the help they can get with us as parents."

There was a moment of comfortable silence as they both sipped their wine, lost in thoughts of the future. Then Emma spoke again, her tone more serious. "Franz, I've been thinking a lot about giving back. I want to do something meaningful with our resources. What if we opened an epilepsy research facility? It's a cause close to your heart."

Franz's eyes softened. "I love that idea. There's so much more we can do to help people with epilepsy. We could fund cutting-edge research, support families, and raise awareness. It could make a real difference."

Emma nodded, feeling a swell of pride and love for the man beside her. "And I want to start a heart health non-profit. My family has a history of heart disease, and I think we could really help with prevention and education."

Franz leaned over and kissed her gently. "You're amazing, you know that? We're going to change the world."

Emma smiled against his lips. "Together, we can do anything."

They shared a tender moment, the intimacy of their dreams binding them even closer. Then Franz pulled back slightly, a mischievous glint in his eye. "So, we agree on the investments, the real estate, the kids' education, and our philanthropic endeavors?"

"Absolutely," Emma replied, her eyes sparkling with determination and love.

"Then it's settled," Franz said, raising his glass once more. "To our future—bold, adventurous, and impactful."

They kissed on it, sealing their plans with a promise. As they stood up to go inside, Emma looked back at the city one last time. "You know," she said with a chuckle, "this is the part where we usually say something profound and then ride off into the sunset."

Franz laughed. "How about we skip the sunset and go watch Netflix instead?"

"Perfect," Emma agreed, her heart full and her spirit light.

Determined to honor Stella's memory and the lessons she had imparted, Emma channeled her grief into creating a storybook for her unborn son, Luc. The book was a modge-podge of her life's journey, filled with tales of courage, transformation, and the enduring power of love. Through this process, Emma found healing and a renewed sense of purpose.

As she crafted each page, Emma was reminded of her own resilience. She had come a long way from the woman who had been haunted by the shadows of her past. She was nothing like her mother, and she wanted Luc to know that he came from a lineage of strength and growth. She defended her past not as a series of mistakes, but as crucial steps in her journey toward becoming the woman she was today.

Franz had always been a rock for Emma, steadfast and supportive. He never let her past haunt their present, treating her history not as a burden but as a tapestry that made her the person he loved. This understanding created a foundation of respect that their relationship thrived on.

One evening, they sat on their terrace, the city lights flickering below like distant stars. The wine glasses between them were almost empty, the conversation easy and flowing.

"Remember when I first told you about my family's history?" Emma asked, a hint of nostalgia in her voice.

Franz chuckled. "How could I forget? You laid it all out like a dramatic novel. It was captivating."

Emma smiled, shaking her head. "I was so nervous. I thought you'd judge me, or worse, leave."

Franz reached out, taking her hand in his. "Never. Your past is part of who you are. And I love every part of you."

They sat in comfortable silence for a moment, the bond between them stronger than ever. It was this mutual respect and honesty that had deepened their relationship, paving the way for genuine trust and intimacy. They spent countless nights like this, discussing their dreams and fears, finding comfort in each other's presence.

But they never grew complacent. They knew that maintaining a healthy relationship required effort and dedication. Franz, in his own quirky way, found a unique method to honor this commitment—and Stella's memory.

Stella had been a force of nature, and her departure had left a void. To keep her spirit alive, Franz developed a tradition that was equal parts homage and inside joke.

"Alright," Franz said one evening, with a mischievous grin, "it's time for our weekly 'Stella Moment.'"

Emma rolled her eyes, laughing. "You and your 'Stella Moments.' What have you got for me this time?"

Franz stood up, clearing his throat dramatically. "Ladies and gentlemen, in honor of the incomparable Stella, a reading from her favorite book of dark humor: 'The Snarky Guide to Living.'"

He pulled out an old, well-worn book from the shelf, one that Stella had loved for its irreverent take on life. Franz began reading a passage about the absurdity of human nature, his delivery perfectly timed to emphasize the sarcasm.

Emma laughed so hard she had tears in her eyes. "You're ridiculous, you know that?"

Franz closed the book, a twinkle in his eye. "Ridiculous, but effective. Stella would have approved."

Emma nodded, wiping her eyes. "She definitely would have. Thank you for this. It means a lot."

Franz sat back down, pulling her into his arms. "It's my way of keeping her spirit alive, and reminding us both not to take life too seriously."

Their nights were filled with these little rituals, blending humor and heart in a way that kept their relationship vibrant. They never let the weight of the world dampen their spirits. Instead, they found ways to laugh, love, and honor those who had touched their lives.

In these moments, they often discussed their future plans with a blend of earnestness and wit.

"Alright," Franz said, his tone mock-serious, "let's talk about our world domination plans. First, we buy up all the real estate in upstate New York. Then, we corner the market on artisanal cheese."

Emma snorted. "And don't forget our investment in cryptocurrency. We'll become the overlords of digital finance."

"Exactly," Franz agreed, eyes twinkling. "But seriously, our plans for the epilepsy research facility and the heart health non-profit are solid. We're going to make a real difference."

Emma kissed him on the cheek. "We are. And we'll do it with humor and grace, just like Stella would have wanted."

Their discussions, though often laced with dark humor, always circled back to their commitment to each other and to their shared goals. They understood that life was unpredictable and sometimes brutal, but they chose to face it together, armed with love and laughter.

One evening, after one of their 'Stella Moments,' they sat quietly, the weight of their plans and dreams settling comfortably around them.

"To us," Emma said softly, raising her glass. "To our absurd, wonderful life."

Franz clinked his glass against hers. "To us. And to always finding the humor in everything, no matter what."

Emma's storybook for Luc became a labor of love, a way to impart wisdom and values to her son. She filled it with stories of her ancestors, the lessons she had learned, and the faith that had guided her through her darkest days. Each story was a piece of her heart, a testament to the strength that had carried her forward.

One evening, as they sat together reviewing the final pages of the storybook, Franz took Emma's hand in his. "This is beautiful, Emma. Luc will grow up knowing where he comes from and the incredible strength within him."

Emma smiled, her eyes glistening with tears. "I want him to know that our past doesn't define us. It's our choices, our faith, and our love that shape who we become."

As the months passed, the bond between Emma and Franz grew stronger, forged in the fires of shared experiences and tempered by their unwavering commitment to each other. They faced the impending arrival of their child, Luc, with a mixture of excitement and determination, their love solidified by the trials they had faced together.

Emma, once restless and discontent, had transformed into a woman of grace and strength. Franz, always supportive and understanding, had evolved alongside her, becoming a pillar of resilience and love. Together, they created a sanctuary of trust and warmth, ready to welcome their son into a world rich with love, faith, and the enduring legacy of his mother's journey.

Emma and Franz nurtured their son with the values they cherished, ensuring he grew up in a stable, upper-class household filled with love and opportunity. Emma thanked her ancestors and Franz daily, her heart overflowing with gratitude for the life they had built together.

As Luc grew older, the storybook became a cherished part of his bedtime routine. He would listen with wide-eyed wonder as Emma read to him, absorbing the tales of courage and transformation. Through these stories, he came to understand the depth of his mother's strength and the unwavering love that bound their family together.

Emma had grown into her role as a formidable housewife and mother, a transformation marked by grace and dedication. She relished the cocoon of luxury that she and Franz had built together, a life filled with comfort, elegance, and the laughter of their son, Luc. Their home was a sanctuary, a testament to their love and hard work.

Every morning, Emma rose with the sun, her heart full of gratitude for the life they had created. She moved through their spacious home with a sense of purpose, ensuring that every detail was perfect. The sprawling gardens were meticulously maintained, the interiors elegantly decorated with a blend of classic and contemporary styles. It was a haven where they could retreat from the world and immerse themselves in the joys of family life.

Emma's days were filled with the responsibilities she had come to embrace with pride. She oversaw the household staff, ensuring that everything ran smoothly. She planned meals that delighted Franz, Clara, and Luc, incorporating the finest ingredients and culinary techniques she had mastered over the years. Her expertise in the kitchen was matched only by her flair for hosting, making every dinner an occasion to remember.

Her dedication extended to Luc's upbringing. She was deeply involved in his education, guiding him through his studies with patience and wisdom. Emma instilled in him the values that had carried her through her own journey: resilience, faith, and the importance of living with integrity. She wanted Luc to grow up understanding the legacy of strength and love that was his birthright.

While Emma managed the household with skill and grace, she also allowed Franz to take the lead in deciding how they spent their time. This partnership worked beautifully for them, as Franz's creativity and vision complemented Emma's practicality and nurturing spirit. He planned their vacations, choosing destinations that offered both relaxation and adventure, and together they created a lifetime of cherished memories.

On a particularly perfect summer day, they found themselves on a pristine beach, the turquoise waves gently lapping at the shore. Franz lay back on a sunlounger, soaking in the sun's warm rays. He wore a contented smile, his eyes closed as he let the serenity of the moment wash over him. Emma watched him from beneath the shade of a wide-brimmed hat, her heart swelling with love and satisfaction.

Luc and Clara played nearby, building elaborate sandcastles with a group of children he had befriended. His laughter mingled with the sound of the waves, a joyful symphony that made Emma's heart sing. She sipped a cool glass of lemonade, the tangy sweetness refreshing in the summer heat. The beach was their haven, a place where they could unwind and reconnect with each other.

Emma joined Franz on the sunlounger, resting her head on his shoulder. He wrapped an arm around her, pulling her close. "This is perfect," he murmured, his voice filled with contentment. "Thank you for everything, Emma."

She smiled, feeling the warmth of his affection. "I should be the one thanking you, Franz. You've given us a beautiful life."

They lay together in comfortable silence, watching Luc's sandcastle grow taller and more intricate. Emma's mind wandered to the journey that had brought them here. She thought of Stella, whose wisdom had set her on the path to transformation. She thought of the faith that had guided her and the love that had sustained her.

They spent the evening together, watching the sunset and enjoying a simple picnic on the beach. The sky turned shades of pink and orange, a breathtaking backdrop to their perfect day. As they packed up to head home, Emma felt a deep sense of fulfillment. She knew that their future was bright, filled with the promise of more beautiful days and cherished moments.

Back at their luxurious home, Emma tucked Luc into bed, reading him a story from the book she had created. His eyes grew heavy, and he drifted off to sleep with a smile on his face. Emma kissed his forehead, whispering a prayer of gratitude for her family.

Emma joined Franz in their bedroom, the soft glow of their bedside lamps casting a warm ambiance around them. They spoke softly about their plans for the next day, their voices a comforting murmur in the quiet of the night. They shared dreams and hopes, discussing their aspirations with a sense of optimism that had grown stronger over the years.

As they lay together, Emma felt a deep sense of contentment and love envelop her. She nestled into Franz's arms, finding solace in his embrace. The stresses of the day melted away as they talked about their future, their laughter mingling with whispered promises.

Emma's quest to understand the enigmatic reference Stella had made about Homais led her on a journey through Yonville again. Emma found herself drawn to Homais' town, yearning to understand the brutality of life and how, despite the chaos and schism, people continued to nurture dreams and bring new life into the world. She walked through the streets, observing the daily struggles and triumphs of ordinary people. The magnitude of their perseverance against the backdrop of a seemingly indifferent universe was both heartbreaking and inspiring.

In her conversations with locals, Emma encountered stories of hardship, loss, and resilience. A woman whose husband had been lost to war, yet who continued to raise their children with unwavering hope. A man who had seen his business crumble but found solace in his family and the promise of a better future. These stories painted a vivid picture of human tenacity, but also of the brutal realities that many faced.

Emma realized that while dreams and new life persisted, they did so in a world fraught with suffering and uncertainty. This realization weighed heavily on her, but it also sparked a glimmer of understanding. There was a solution, she thought, but it was not one that had been directly expressed or celebrated. It was the quiet resilience of individuals, the uncelebrated acts of kindness, and the enduring hope that lay at the heart of human existence. The understanding that there would always be another problem money could help solve ran through her mind.

As she sat on the beach, watching Franz soak in the sun, Emma's thoughts turned to the future. Franz's recent move to embrace modern technology in his work resonated deeply with her own desire to steer the world toward a more positive direction. She saw in his innovations a beacon of hope, a way to harness the chaos and channel it into progress and improvement. She knew she couldn't do it all, but she was grateful for everything she was capable of.

Franz's endeavors in modern technology were ambitious, aiming to create sustainable solutions and bridge the divides that plagued society. Emma encouraged him onward, feeling a surge of pride and a sense of purpose. She supported his vision wholeheartedly, becoming his confidante and cheerleader. Their partnership evolved, with Emma playing an instrumental role in shaping the direction of their collective efforts.

Emma's sense of fulfillment grew as she became more involved in Franz's work. She felt like a superstar, her influence and ideas helping to drive meaningful change. Yet, as she reveled in their successes, she also became increasingly disillusioned with the struggles that still permeated the world around her. The dichotomy between their privileged existence and the harsh realities faced by so many others was stark.

Raising Luc and Clara in their stable, upper-class household, Emma was acutely aware of the advantages they enjoyed. She wanted to shield him from the brutality of life, but also to instill in him a sense of empathy and responsibility. Despite their cocoon of luxury, Emma could not escape the nagging discontent that came with witnessing the world's struggles. She began to question whether their efforts were enough, whether they were truly making a difference. This disillusionment was a stark contrast to the optimism she had felt earlier, but it also fueled her determination to do more.

Emma's inner conflict reached a turning point one evening as she sat with Franz, discussing their plans. She expressed her doubts and fears, her voice tinged with frustration. "We're doing so much, yet it feels like a drop in the ocean. There's so much suffering, so much we can't control."

Franz took her hand, his gaze steady and reassuring. "Emma, we can't change the world overnight. But every small step, every positive change, matters. We're creating a legacy for Luc and Clara, and that's something to be proud of."

His words resonated with her, reminding her of the quiet resilience she had witnessed in Homais' town. Emma realized that while they might not solve all the world's problems, their efforts were not in vain. They were part of a larger call for change, contributing to a future where dreams could thrive amidst chaos.

Emma sat Clara and Luc down in the living room, a serious expression on her face despite the lighthearted topic she intended to discuss.

"Kids," she began, "today we're going to talk about something very important—respecting all living creatures, even the ones that might annoy us."

Clara and Luc exchanged curious glances, wondering what their mother was getting at.

Emma continued, "Let's take spiders, for example. Sometimes, we find them in the bathroom or crawling around the house. They might startle us or seem creepy, but they're actually very helpful."

Luc wrinkled his nose, remembering the time a spider had startled him in the bathroom.

"Spiders eat other bugs," Emma explained, "like mosquitoes and flies. They help keep our home free from pests, almost like tiny pest control experts."

Clara nodded thoughtfully, imagining the spider as a superhero battling insects.

"Now," Emma continued, "if you see a spider or any other creature that's bothering you, remember they're just trying to live their lives, too. We should try to gently guide them outside or leave them alone, rather than harm them."

Luc scratched his head, considering his usual reaction to spiders.

Emma smiled warmly, "Remember, every creature—even the smallest ones—has a place in our world. By respecting them, we're showing kindness and compassion, which are traits that make us better people."

Clara raised her hand, "But what if they're really scary?"

Emma chuckled softly, "I understand it can be scary sometimes. That's why we can calmly ask for help to relocate them. Daddy or I can always lend a hand if you're feeling nervous."

Luc nodded, feeling reassured by his mom's words.

"Okay, Mom," Clara said with determination, "we'll be kind to all the creatures, even the ones that scare us."

Emma beamed with pride, knowing her children were beginning to understand the importance of empathy and respect for all living beings. As they went about their day, she felt a sense of accomplishment in teaching them this valuable lesson—one that would shape their attitudes and actions towards the natural world for years to come.

Franz's words echoed in Emma's mind as they strolled through a hidden garden, a sanctuary tucked away from the hustle and bustle of their everyday lives. "Living an amazing life is the best revenge," he had told her, his voice tinged with determination and a hint of mischief. Emma couldn't help but smile as she reflected on the truth of his words.

Emma had come a long way since her days of turmoil and uncertainty. She had found a balance in her life that she had once thought impossible—a balance between ambition and contentment, between dreams and reality. Franz's unwavering support and love had been a beacon of strength, guiding her through the darkest moments and celebrating her victories, both big and small.

As they wandered through the garden, Franz stopped to pluck a vibrant flower, tucking it behind Emma's ear with a tender smile. "You deserve all the beauty in the world," he whispered, his eyes full of adoration.

They sat on a bench overlooking a tranquil pond, the sounds of nature enveloping them in a peaceful serenity. Franz recited poetry that spoke to their shared journey—the highs and lows, the laughter and tears. Emma listened, her heart swelling with love and appreciation for the man who had transformed her life in ways she had never imagined.

In Franz's arms, Emma felt safe and cherished. His love was a constant source of strength, empowering her to embrace her passions and pursue her dreams with unwavering determination. Together, they were building a future filled with promise and possibility, a testament to their enduring bond and shared vision.

Later that evening, as they returned home, Emma felt a sense of optimism about her abilities and her future. Franz had taught her that living an amazing life wasn't just about success or recognition—it was about finding joy in the everyday moments, cherishing the love of family and friends, and embracing the journey, however unpredictable it may be.

They settled into their expansive living room, the soft glow of candlelight casting a warm ambiance. Franz pulled out a book of poetry, reading aloud verses that spoke to their shared hopes and dreams. Emma nestled beside him, feeling a deep sense of contentment and gratitude.

Afterwards, Emma sat Clara and Luc down at the kitchen table, their iPads nestled in front of them like sacred relics of the digital age. She took a deep breath, preparing herself for the task ahead—teaching her children the delicate art of navigating social media responsibly.

"Alright, you two," Emma began, her tone a mix of authority and lightheartedness, "social media is like a crowded street. There are nice people, weirdos, and sometimes, people who think they're cats. Your job is to be street smart."

Clara, wide-eyed and eager to learn, nodded solemnly. Luc, already scrolling through cat memes, looked up with mild interest.

"First rule," Emma continued, "never post anything you wouldn't want Grandma to see. Once it's out there, it's like glitter in the carpet—impossible to clean up."

Luc chuckled, imagining Grandma scrolling through his hypothetical meme stash. Clara scribbled notes on a napkin, determined to remember every word of her mother's wisdom.

"Second," Emma continued, "beware of trolls. They're like real-life grumpy garden gnomes, hiding under bridges waiting to ruin your day. Ignore them or block them—your choice."

Luc nodded, his finger hovering over the block button as he imagined himself vanquishing internet trolls like a digital superhero.

"And third," Emma added with a serious tone, "don't believe everything you see. People on social media can make their lives look perfect, but it's often just a highlight reel. Real life is messy, like your rooms on a Saturday morning."

Clara and Luc exchanged knowing glances, silently admitting their rooms often resembled war zones more than Pinterest boards.

"As for privacy," Emma concluded, "guard yours like a dragon guards treasure. Never share personal information or your location with strangers."

Luc and Clara nodded in unison, their minds buzzing with newfound knowledge and caution. Emma smiled, proud of her mini social media Jedi apprentices.

"Now," she said, rising from the table, "time for a quiz. What do you do if someone asks for your address online?"

Luc raised his hand eagerly. "Block them and tell you!"

"Good job," Emma praised, ruffling his hair. Clara grinned, feeling empowered by her newfound social media savvy.

As they dispersed to their rooms, Emma couldn't help but chuckle. Teaching social media responsibility was like teaching them to ride a bike—equal parts nerve-wracking and exhilarating. But with a mix of dark humor and wisdom, she knew her children were on the right path to mastering the digital landscape—one meme at a time.

Emma had come to understand that independence and fulfillment were not mutually exclusive from love and partnership. In a world where women had more opportunities than ever before, she realized that the desire for companionship, support, and shared experiences transcended societal expectations or stereotypes.

Franz had shown her the beauty and strength of a partnership built on mutual respect, love, and shared dreams. He had enriched her life in ways she had never imagined, offering companionship that complemented her independence rather than defining it. Their relationship was a testament to the possibility of having it all—not as a checklist of achievements, but as a soft blanket woven with love, understanding, and growth.

Emma had faced the hard truths of life with courage and resilience, embracing the challenges as opportunities for growth rather than setbacks. The world's unpredictability and the inherent nature of human existence had tested her resolve, yet she had emerged stronger and more determined. The struggles she had witnessed—the pain, the loss, and the resilience of ordinary people—had inspired her to make a difference, to contribute positively to the world around her. Franz's unwavering optimism and belief in making a meaningful impact had fueled her own sense of purpose, guiding her toward initiatives and endeavors that aimed to create a brighter future for all.

As she sat with Franz on their balcony, overlooking the city bathed in the glow of twilight, Emma found solace in the complexities of life. She knew that while challenges would continue to shape their journey, their love and partnership would remain steadfast. Together, they would navigate the uncertainties of the world, finding strength in each other's presence and celebrating the beauty of living a life filled with love, purpose, and shared dreams.

In a world where independence and inspiration intertwined, Emma had found her answers—not in absolutes or definitive conclusions, but in the evolving narrative of her own life, guided by love, resilience, and the pursuit of a meaningful existence.

Their story was not just about Emma or Franz—it was a celebration of the human spirit, of the limitless possibilities that emerged when love and independence walked hand in hand, inspiring hope and shaping the future. And as Emma closed the chapter on her reflections, she knew that their journey was far from over—a journey filled with love, laughter, and the endless possibilities that awaited them on the horizon.

In the midst of a world filled with contentious politics, sensitive ethical dilemmas, and rapidly changing cultural norms, Emma found herself grappling with profound questions about the future she wanted to create for her children and the world they would inherit. As Emma strolled through the bustling streets of the city, she couldn't help but chuckle at the ironies that unfolded around her like scenes from a quirky sitcom.

First, she passed by a high-end gym where fitness enthusiasts lined up to pay hefty membership fees for the privilege of running on treadmills and lifting weights indoors, all while the sun shone brightly outside for free. Emma imagined nature rolling its eyes at this peculiar human behavior.

Next, she encountered a group of protesters passionately advocating for environmental sustainability while sipping coffee from disposable cups and checking their smartphones every few minutes. The irony was not lost on Emma — fighting for a greener planet while contributing to single-use waste and electronic consumption.

Further down the street, she spotted a vegan restaurant with a sign boasting about its sustainable, plant-based menu. Just beside it, however, was a fast-food joint emitting the irresistible aroma of fried chicken, its patrons indulging in greasy meals without a care for the carbon footprint.

As Emma waited to cross a busy intersection, she witnessed a scene that could only happen in a city: a businessman in an expensive suit arguing loudly on his Bluetooth headset about financial projections, oblivious to the street performer beside him playing a soulful tune on a beat-up guitar for spare change.

Passing by a trendy art gallery, Emma observed patrons sipping champagne and discussing the profound meanings behind abstract paintings, while a few blocks away, street artists created vibrant murals on abandoned walls, hoping for a fraction of the recognition and none of the champagne.

The day culminated in a visit to a bustling farmers' market where vendors proudly displayed organic produce and homemade goods, each stall adorned with eco-friendly signs. Yet, the parking lot overflowed with gas-guzzling SUVs, their drivers loading up on fresh vegetables before zooming off to suburban homes miles away.

Emma couldn't help but smile at the quirks and contradictions of city life, where ideals clashed with realities, and every corner held a surprise or a punchline waiting to be discovered. Amidst the chaos and contradictions, she found a strange comfort in the comedic absurdity of it all, knowing that life in the city would always keep her on her toes and provide ample material for reflection and amusement.

In a world driven by consumerism and instant gratification, Emma was deeply troubled by the marketing of fast abortions and the disposable nature of fast fashion. She instilled in her children a sense of environmental stewardship and ethical consumption, teaching them to value sustainability, ethical sourcing, and conscious living. Emma encouraged critical reflection on the impact of consumer choices on global communities and the environment, empowering her children to make informed decisions that aligned with their values and principles.

As she sat with her children, engaging in thoughtful discussions about ethics, morality, and their role in shaping a better world, Emma felt a sense of hope and purpose. She knew that by imparting values of kindness, justice, and respect, she was preparing her children to navigate the complexities of the modern world with courage and conviction.

It was all so overwhelming that one evening, the entire family collapsed into bed like a troop of exhausted soldiers after a battle with an army of toddlers armed with crayons. Franz, Emma, Clara and Luc, each tucked under their mountain of blankets, dreamed sweet dreams about their futures together—Franz imagining a world where he finally perfected his recipe for avocado toast that Clara couldn't resist, and Luc envisioning a future where his mastery of Legos earned him the title of "Lego King of the Universe."

Meanwhile, Emma dreamed of a utopia where the dishes magically washed themselves and the laundry folded itself into perfectly crisp stacks. In this dream, she and Franz effortlessly managed their investments in crypto and real estate while simultaneously running their children's private education fund and spearheading groundbreaking research in epilepsy and heart health. It was a ludicrously blissful scenario where chaos turned into comedy and stress morphed into slapstick.

As they snored gently in unison, the power of togetherness and unity filled the room like a thick fog of contentment, smothering any lingering anxieties and worries. The family slept soundly, their dreams adorned with a sprinkling of dark humor that made even the most daunting challenges of life seem like scenes from a sitcom they couldn't help but laugh along with.

As the mother, Emma knew she would be the ringleader of the next day—a role she embraced with both determination and a touch of trepidation. She could almost feel her mothers looking down on her from Heaven, their celestial applause echoing in her heart. Their guidance and love seemed to guide her steps as she navigated the challenges of raising a family while balancing her own dreams and ambitions.

Emma gathered Clara and Luc in the kitchen, a place she deemed the heart of their home's environmental education. She had a mischievous glint in her eye, ready to impart wisdom with a dash of humor about conserving electricity and water.

"Alright, kiddos," Emma began, holding up a bright yellow energy-saving light bulb like a trophy, "today we're diving into the thrilling world of saving electricity and water. Think of it like a game of 'Don't Make Mom Turn Green!'"

Clara giggled, while Luc raised an eyebrow, intrigued by the challenge.

"First rule," Emma declared, "if you're not in the room, turn off the light. Pretend the light switch is your best friend—it's always there when you need it, but you don't leave it hanging!"

Luc nodded, imagining his light switch as a faithful sidekick in the battle against wasted electricity.

"And," Emma continued, "when you brush your teeth, remember—tap dancing with the faucet is fun, but we're not auditioning for 'Water's Got Talent.' Keep it off until you're rinsing."

Clara mimed a dramatic faucet tap dance, making her mother chuckle.

"Next," Emma said with a sly grin, "let's talk about laundry. You know those jeans you wear once and toss in the laundry like they're on vacation? Well, they're not. They need a staycation in your closet for a bit longer."

Luc nodded solemnly, already envisioning his jeans lounging by the wardrobe poolside.

Emma continued, "Oh, and showers! A quick rinse is like a lightning round in a game show—keep it under five minutes, and you'll win the water conservation jackpot!"

Clara giggled, imagining herself showering at breakneck speed to avoid the imaginary game show buzzer.

"As for gadgets," Emma added, "let's unplug those vampires! You know, the chargers and appliances sucking electricity even when they're not in use. They're like sneaky vampires trying to drain our energy!"

Luc chuckled, imagining a tiny vampire sucking on his phone charger.

"And lastly," Emma concluded, "let's be eco-savvy superheroes. Every little switch-off and water drip saved adds up to big wins for our planet. So, who's ready to join the Conservation Crusaders?"

Clara and Luc exchanged excited glances, eager to embark on their mission to save the world, one light switch and faucet tap at a time.

As they dispersed to put their newfound knowledge into action, Emma leaned back with a satisfied smile. Teaching conservation with humor and wisdom was like planting seeds of responsibility and environmental stewardship in their young minds—seeds that she knew would grow into a future where they'd make their mom proud, one energy-efficient step at a time.

Her days were no longer a mere routine but a canvas waiting to be painted with purpose and meaning. From managing the household to nurturing Luc's curiosity and Franz's entrepreneurial spirit, Emma found fulfillment in every moment. Each decision she made carried the weight of responsibility but also the promise of shaping a brighter future for her loved ones.

With a mix of nostalgia and gratitude, Emma reflected on how far she had come—from the restless young woman grappling with uncertainties to the confident matriarch leading her family with grace. She knew that her journey was intertwined with those who had come before her, and she carried their legacy forward with pride.

Emma had once felt like an outsider in Brooklyn, unsure if she would ever truly belong. But as time passed and she embraced her role as a community leader, things began to change. Brooklyn, known for its vibrant and diverse culture, had a way of welcoming those who showed genuine care and commitment.

One sunny morning, Emma strolled down the familiar streets of her neighborhood, greeted warmly by shopkeepers and neighbors alike. Gone were the days of feeling like an outsider; now, she was Momma Bovary, respected and admired.

At the McDonald's drive-thru, she observed obese individuals squeezed into their cars, their vehicles straining under the weight of their occupants. The allure of fast food beckoned, offering quick and convenient sustenance amidst the daily rush. Yet, alongside them, on street corners and benches, homeless individuals were glued to their phones. These devices, perhaps their only connection to the world beyond their circumstances, held them captive in a digital realm while their physical reality remained harsh and unforgiving.

The juxtaposition was striking: those with means to afford fast food found themselves physically struggling, while those without a roof over their heads found solace or escape in the digital world. Emma pondered the societal irony — the availability of excess and indulgence juxtaposed with the harsh realities of poverty and isolation.

It was a sobering reminder of the complexities of modern life, where technology and consumerism often coexist with stark inequality and social disconnect. Emma's thoughts lingered on the profound challenges facing society, where access to basic needs and the allure of digital distraction intertwined in unexpected ways, painting a poignant picture of contemporary urban life.

Throughout the day, Emma noticed the perks of being embraced by her neighbors. There were no traffic jams when she drove through the bustling streets, no heckling or harassment from passersby. At the grocery store, she breezed through checkout without waiting in line, and even at the zoo, she enjoyed the exhibits in peace and quiet.

Reflecting on these moments, Emma couldn't help but feel a sense of satisfaction. She had made choices to engage with her community, to contribute positively, and to lead by example. The respect she received was not just for her name but for the values she stood for and the way she treated others.

As she sipped her latte and watched the world go by, Emma knew she had found her place in Brooklyn. She was not just an observer but an active participant in making her community a better place—one smile and one positive interaction at a time.

Life with Franz turned out just right. She didn't know it when she entered City Hall that autumn, but she knew it now. It was far from boring and she was far from a pawn in her own life. Her superficial desires were replaced by resonating values and that moral compass led her to the life of her dreams.

Emma reflected on Madame Bovary's tumultuous journey, imagining if she could rewrite her own story. Sitting at her desk, she scribbled a note to herself, a mantra born from her own experiences and aspirations:

"Live for your children. Live for your future."

It wasn't just a simple reminder; it was a declaration of intent. Emma had learned the hard way about the consequences of chasing fleeting desires and ignoring the deeper responsibilities and joys that life offered. Madame Bovary's cautionary tale echoed in her mind, urging her to prioritize what truly mattered.

She thought about Clara and Luc, her greatest treasures, and the future she wanted to build for them. Emma envisioned a life filled with love, stability, and meaningful connections—a stark contrast to the impulsive pursuits of her past. She wanted her children to learn from her mistakes and embrace the values that would guide them to fulfillment.

As she sealed the note and placed it in a drawer, Emma felt a sense of peace wash over her. Madame Bovary's legacy had taught her that life's greatest treasures weren't found in material indulgence or reckless passion, but in the enduring bonds of family and the promise of a better tomorrow.

Franz had always been keenly aware of Emma's heritage, the whispers that trailed her name, and the unspoken fears that lurked in the shadows of their community. He knew of the lingering stigma attached to the Bovary name, born from the tragic tales of generations past. Yet, Franz chose not to burden Emma with these dark histories. Instead, he saw beyond the rumors and judgments, straight to Emma's heart.

He admired her resilience, her boundless compassion, and the genuine laughter that lit up a room. Franz found solace in Emma's presence, her warmth becoming a beacon of light in his own life. While others whispered and speculated, Franz quietly supported Emma, nurturing her growth and celebrating her victories.

Their love flourished in the quiet moments, away from the prying eyes of society. Franz cherished Emma's every smile, her unwavering spirit, and the depth of her love for their children. He understood the weight of her past and the importance of allowing her to forge her own path, free from the shadows that haunted her ancestors.

As they navigated life together, Franz admired Emma's transformation into a woman of grace and strength. He found himself in awe of her ability to rise above adversity, to embrace life with a fierce determination that inspired everyone around her. And in the intimacy of their shared moments, Franz silently thanked fate for bringing Emma into his life, knowing that her heart was pure and her love was the greatest gift he could ever receive.

Franz often found himself chuckling at the profound ironies that life presented. As he and Emma sat in their cozy living room, sipping on herbal tea and discussing their children's latest achievements, the television hummed softly in the background, broadcasting news of conflicts raging across distant lands.

On the screen, reporters in flak jackets delivered updates from war-torn regions, where cities lay in ruins and civilians endured unimaginable hardships. Images of tanks rolling through rubble-strewn streets and distraught families seeking refuge flashed before their eyes, stark contrasts to the peace and comfort of their suburban sanctuary.

Franz couldn't help but marvel at the absurdity of it all — how the wealthiest and most influential individuals on the planet vied for power and influence, their actions shaping global policies and economies, while everyday people like him and Emma focused on mundane tasks like grocery shopping and weekend barbecues.

"It's like we're living in two different worlds," Franz mused, his voice tinged with both amusement and disbelief. "Here we are, worried about which color to paint the kitchen walls, while half a world away, people are fighting for their lives."

Emma nodded thoughtfully, her gaze shifting from the flickering images on the screen to the warmth of their family photos adorning the walls. "It's surreal, isn't it?" she replied softly. "We're so insulated from all that chaos, yet it's happening right now, shaping the future of our world."

They sat in silence for a moment, contemplating the vast disparities and injustices that existed beyond their suburban haven. Outside, the neighborhood children played on well-manicured lawns, their laughter mingling with the distant echoes of sirens from emergency vehicles rushing by.

"I guess that's life," Franz said finally, breaking the silence with a wry smile. "The absurdity of it all. The rich and powerful maneuvering over a world in turmoil, while we sit here, trying to make sense of it from our comfortable living room."

Emma reached out and took his hand, squeezing it gently. "At least we're aware," she said, her voice tinged with a mix of gratitude and determination. "And we can teach our children to see beyond the surface, to understand the complexities of our world, and to strive for compassion and understanding."

Franz nodded, feeling a renewed sense of purpose. As they watched the news together, their conversation shifted to how they could contribute positively to the world, starting with their own community and extending outward. Amidst the irony and chaos of global affairs, they found solace in their ability to make a difference, however small, in the lives of those around them.

In the quiet expanse of their bedroom, Franz, the illustrious leader of prestigious funds and awards, found solace in the warmth of Emma's presence. The evening air was thick with a sense of reverence and desire, mingling with the faint scent of jasmine from the nearby garden.

As they embraced, their connection transcended the boundaries of mere physicality. Franz, a titan in the world of finance and medicine, surrendered to Emma with a tender fervor that spoke of deep admiration and unspoken understanding. Emma, radiant in the moonlight streaming through the window, reciprocated his passion with a grace that bespoke years of shared moments and unbreakable trust.

In that intimate space, where their worlds converged and barriers melted away, they made love with a profound blend of power and passion, each heartbeat echoing the rhythm of their unspoken vows and the promise of a future entwined in mutual respect and boundless love.

In a quaint suburban church tucked away from the bustling city, Pastor Hank stood at the pulpit, his voice booming with fervor as he preached to his congregation about the importance of compassion and forgiveness. The pews were filled with devout parishioners nodding in agreement, their hymnals open to verses of love and redemption.

"Now, brothers and sisters," Pastor Hank proclaimed, his hands raised dramatically, "we must remember that even the most wayward among us are deserving of a second chance! Just as our Lord forgives, so must we extend our grace to those who have stumbled."

As the congregation murmured their affirmations, a small group of church volunteers huddled in a corner, preparing for their weekly outreach program at the local prison. They diligently packed boxes of toiletries and bibles, ready to bring hope and support to inmates seeking spiritual guidance and rehabilitation.

Meanwhile, across town in the bustling city center, a different kind of sermon was unfolding. Mayor Beverly, known for her fiery rhetoric and uncompromising stance on city policies, addressed a crowd of protesters gathered outside City Hall. Her voice carried over the crowd as she championed her latest initiative to overhaul public transportation, despite widespread opposition from reluctant citizens.

"We will not be deterred by naysayers!" Mayor Beverly declared, her fist pumping in the air. "Progress requires bold action, and I will not rest until our city's infrastructure meets the needs of every resident!"

In the midst of the fervor, a group of bewildered tourists wandered by, snapping photos of the scene with puzzled expressions. Nearby, a street performer dressed as a clown juggled brightly colored balls, adding an unintentional layer of surrealism to the chaotic tableau.

And somewhere in the middle, amidst the clash of ideals and the swirl of city life, a quirky harmony emerged—a reminder that in the tapestry of human endeavor, irony often weaves the threads of understanding and resilience.

Franz and Emma just laughed to each other as they continued trying to create peace that never seemed to last long. That, in and of itself, was the ride of a lifetime. It never got boring because just as one would become complicit or complacent, the other would nudge them awake and onward, creating positive vibrations the other could count on.

"So what's for dinner?" Franz asked lightheartedly.

Emma loved his mind, and when she realized there was no right way to parent, a huge weight lifted off of her shoulders. She did not end up becoming a famous politician, a world-renowned anything, or a prophet. No, Emma became herself. In a world full of desires and distractions, the desire to become the best version of herself was the only one worth striving for.

Franz sat at the worn, wooden kitchen table of their Brooklyn brownstone, the morning light filtering through the curtains casting delicate patterns on the walls. The sounds of the bustling city outside were a stark contrast to the quietude within their home. Emma bustled around the kitchen, her movements swift and purposeful as she prepared breakfast. The aroma of freshly brewed coffee and warm croissants filled the air, a small nod to their French roots in the heart of New York.

"Emma," Franz began, his voice tentative as he looked up from his coffee cup. "I've been thinking... about our future, about the children's future."

Emma paused, turning to look at him with a curious tilt of her head. "What about it, Franz?"

He sighed, running a hand through his hair. "Brooklyn has been good to us, but I can't help but feel that it might be time for a change. A quieter life, perhaps. Somewhere the children can grow up surrounded by nature, and where we can reconnect with our roots."

Emma's eyes softened as she moved to sit across from him. "You mean France, don't you?"

Franz nodded, his gaze dropping to the table. "Yes. The idea of moving back to the countryside, to where it all began, it feels right. But... I know it won't be easy. And I can't help but feel embarrassed, Emma. You've done so much, provided so much for this family. It feels like I'm failing in my duties as a husband and father."

Emma reached out, taking his hand in hers. "Franz, you have nothing to be embarrassed about. We are a team, and we've both made sacrifices for our family. Moving to France could be a wonderful new chapter for us. A chance for a fresh start, away from the chaos of the city."

Franz looked up, meeting her eyes. "Do you really think so?"

Emma smiled warmly. "I do. And besides, it's not like we'll be starting from scratch. The estate is there, waiting for us. A place where we can build new memories and give our children the kind of upbringing we always wanted for them."

A sense of relief washed over Franz as he squeezed her hand. "Thank you, Emma. For always believing in us, in me. I promise, I'll do everything I can to make this work."

And so, the decision was made. Over the next few weeks, the family began to prepare for their move. The children, Clara and Luc, were excited about the adventure that lay ahead, their young minds filled with images of vast fields and ancient forests. Emma and Franz worked tirelessly to pack up their life in Brooklyn, selling off what they didn't need and arranging for the rest to be shipped overseas.

The day they left Brooklyn was bittersweet. They stood on the stoop of their brownstone, taking one last look at the home that had seen so many of their joys and sorrows. Emma felt a pang of nostalgia as she remembered the early days of their marriage, the struggles and triumphs that had shaped them into the family they were now.

The journey to France was long but filled with anticipation. As their plane descended into Paris, Franz looked out the window, his heart swelling with a mix of pride and hope. This was a new beginning, a chance to build a life that honored their past while embracing their future.

They arrived at the estate late in the afternoon. The grand house stood proudly amidst rolling hills and lush vineyards, its stone walls glowing in the soft light of the setting sun. Emma and Franz exchanged a glance, both feeling a deep sense of rightness about their decision.

As they stepped inside, the children ran ahead, their laughter echoing through the spacious halls. Emma and Franz followed, taking in the familiar yet rejuvenated surroundings. The house was filled with potential, a canvas on which they could paint their dreams.

Franz took Emma's hand, pulling her close. "Welcome home," he whispered, pressing a kiss to her forehead.

"Home," Emma echoed, her eyes shining with tears of happiness. "It feels so good to be home."

Over the following months, they settled into their new life with grace and dignity. Franz found fulfillment in working the land, reviving the vineyards, and managing the estate. Emma continued her seamstress business, her designs gaining popularity among the local gentry. Together, they created a life that balanced the tranquility of the countryside with the sophistication they had cultivated in the city.

The ancestral home in Colmar turned out to be a treasure trove of history and potential. Emma and Franz dedicated themselves to restoring the estate, breathing new life into its ancient walls. The house, once a haunting reminder of a bygone era, now stood as a symbol of their shared dreams and hard work. Each room they renovated brought them closer together, and each discovery they made—a hidden room, a forgotten artifact—added to the rich aesthetics of their lives. The once-dilapidated walls were restored to their former glory, adorned with elegant stonework and lush ivy. The gardens, meticulously tended to, burst with color, showcasing an array of roses, lavender, and hydrangeas. Fountains gurgled softly, adding a serene soundtrack to the idyllic scene.

Inside the grand estate, Emma moved gracefully through the kitchen, her every step a picture of elegance. She wore a simple yet stylish linen dress, its pristine white fabric contrasting beautifully with her bronzed skin. Her hair was loosely tied back, allowing a few wisps to frame her face as she worked. The kitchen itself was a blend of old-world charm and modern convenience, with gleaming marble countertops and rustic wooden beams overhead.

Emma hummed softly to herself as she squeezed fresh lemons into a pitcher, the tart scent mingling with the floral notes wafting in from the open windows. She added a generous amount of sugar and a splash of sparkling water, stirring the concoction with a long wooden spoon. As she worked, her gaze occasionally drifted to the lawn outside, where her two children, Clara and Luc, played with boundless energy.

Clara, the elder of the two, chased her younger brother around the expansive lawn, their laughter ringing out like a joyful symphony. Dressed in crisp white play clothes, they were the epitome of carefree childhood. Their golden curls caught the sunlight as they darted between the neatly trimmed hedges and ancient oak trees, their games a blend of imagination and delight.

Franz, meanwhile, was ensconced in his study, a room that exuded sophistication and power. The walls were lined with dark mahogany bookshelves filled with leather-bound volumes, and a massive oak desk dominated the center of the room. Franz sat in a high-backed leather chair, his posture relaxed yet commanding. He wore a tailored suit, its deep navy fabric perfectly complementing his polished appearance.

On his desk, a sleek laptop was open, displaying a video conference with several important figures from the business world. Franz spoke with authority and confidence, his voice smooth and measured as he discussed the latest developments in his many ventures. He had become a man of great influence, his efforts spanning various industries from technology to philanthropy.

As he listened to a colleague outline a proposal, Franz's eyes flicked momentarily to a framed photograph on his desk. It was a picture of Emma, Clara, and Luc taken during a recent family vacation to the French Riviera. The image captured a moment of pure happiness, a reminder of the rich, fulfilling life he had built with Emma.

Back in the kitchen, Emma poured the freshly made lemonade into tall, crystal glasses. She arranged them on a silver tray alongside a plate of delicate madeleines, their buttery scent mingling with the citrusy aroma of the lemonade. She carried the tray out to the terrace, where a wrought-iron table and chairs were set up under a large, white parasol.

"Children, lemonade's ready!" Emma called out, her voice carrying across the lawn.

Clara and Luc immediately abandoned their game and ran toward the terrace, their faces flushed with excitement. Emma handed each of them a glass, watching with a smile as they took eager sips.

"Maman, it's delicious!" Clara exclaimed, her eyes sparkling with delight.

Luc nodded enthusiastically, a faint mustache of lemonade forming on his upper lip. Emma laughed softly, wiping it away with a gentle hand.

Franz finished his call and joined them on the terrace, his presence commanding yet warm. He bent down to kiss Emma on the cheek, his touch tender and loving.

"How was the call?" Emma asked, handing him a glass of lemonade.

"Productive," Franz replied, taking a sip. "But not as refreshing as this."

Emma smiled, feeling a deep sense of contentment. Their life together had become a perfect blend of luxury and simplicity, ambition and family. They had transformed Antonie's estate into a haven, a place where their children could grow up surrounded by beauty and love.

As the sun began to set, casting a warm, golden light over the estate, Emma and Franz sat together on the terrace, watching Clara and Luc play. They held hands, their fingers intertwined, a silent ode to their enduring bond. The world had a funny way of sorting itself out, Emma mused as she stood on the balcony of her new home, overlooking the lush French countryside. The air was crisp and clean, carrying the scent of lavender and fresh grass. Birds chirped merrily in the trees, and a gentle breeze rustled the leaves, whispering secrets of peace and tranquility. It was a stark contrast to the chaos and uncertainty that had once dominated her life.

In the quiet hours before dawn's first light, a mother wakes, her heart a steady drum, with tender hands, she sets the world aright, though dreams and hopes, for now, remain unsung.

She treads the path of selfless, silent grace, her sacrifices etched in time unseen, in every line of care upon her face, a testament to all that might have been.

Ironies entwine like vines in spring, a world that praises freedom binds her tight, for every triumph, subtle sorrows cling, in shadows cast by joy, there lurks the night.

She learns to choose her battles with a heart that beats with wisdom, tempered by the years, to fight for love, but sometimes to depart, from fights that only yield unspoken tears.

The laundry pile, a mountain, never climbed, the echoes of her laughter, soft and low, in moments missed, her soul becomes resigned, yet in her eyes, a fierce, enduring glow.

For every lullaby and whispered prayer, she knows the worth of choosing when to fight, in every tear, the strength to simply care, she finds the courage to embrace the light.

Her sacrifice, a silent, endless song, a melody that carries through the night, in ironies, she finds where she belongs, and in her battles, chooses love and right.

Too often she is cast down, overlooked, or forgotten. Then, the world can carry the same fate begotten. A mother's love is ever near, a guiding force to embrace and fear.

The majesty of her love shall conquer all hearts, brave or not. It was not the trials and tribulations to blame at all; at the end we were all glad we fought. Cheers, to our uplifting and not the fall.

Don't miss out!

Visit the website below and you can sign up to receive emails whenever Jodi Chow publishes a new book. There's no charge and no obligation.

https://books2read.com/r/B-A-LMKKB-CHUPD

BOOKS 2 READ

Connecting independent readers to independent writers.

Did you love *Urban Desires*? Then you should read *Lady Frankenstein*[1] by Jodi Chow!

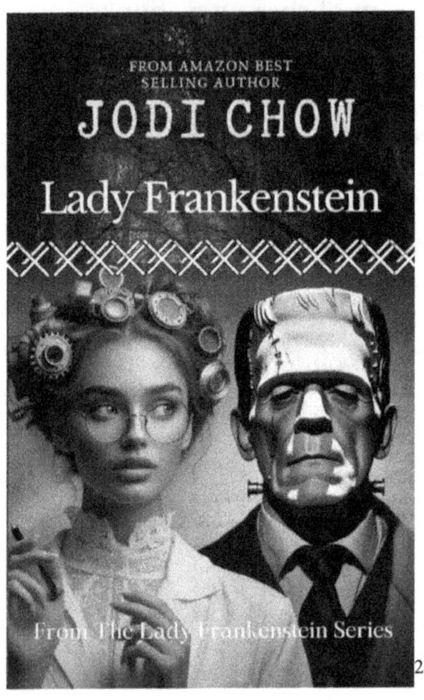

[2]

Pick up where the original Frankenstein left off with Lady Frankenstein. Walton is stuck in the North Pole and has just witnessed the death of Frankenstein. He writes to Margaret and requests that she go and visit Victor's family in Geneva. She leaves her fancy life in London to travel to a gothic estate where lonely and forgotten Frankenstein family members reside.Margaret's daughter, Sonia, tags along for the journey. At the Frankenstein estate, she falls in love with Frankenstein's nephew, Frederick. He is a brooding young man who also happens to be dangerously handsome. Will Sonia leave it all behind for love? Will Victor's reputation tarnish the bright future Margaret had planned for her only daughter?This historical romance

---

1. https://books2read.com/u/4EzGle

2. https://books2read.com/u/4EzGle

is set in the early 1800's and has details that will leave you feeling morbidly haunted. A must read!

Also by Jodi Chow

Isadora Bolt
Lady Frankenstein
Pilgrim's Pie
White Rabbit
Surviving Erica
Christmas Angel Island
Groomed for Love, Lost in Cairo
Isle of Eros
Married To The Warlock
Doodle Duke
Urban Desires
Keeping Up With The Classics Anthology
The Love Story Anthology
The Haunting at Cumberland Arena

www.ingramcontent.com/pod-product-compliance
Lightning Source LLC
Chambersburg PA
CBHW060933140726

47996CB00001B/480